The Birthday Ball

The Birthday Ball

Lois Lowry

Illustrations by Jules Feiffer

Houghton Mifflin Books for Children
HOUGHTON MIFFLIN HARCOURT
BOSTON   NEW YORK   2010

Houghton Mifflin Books for Children is an imprint of
Houghton Mifflin Harcourt Publishing Company.

www.hmhbooks.com

The text of this book is set in Youbee.
The illustrations are pen and ink.

Library of Congress Cataloging-in-Publication Data
Lowry, Lois.
Birthday ball / by Lois Lowry ; illustrated by Jules Feiffer.
p. cm.
Summary: When a bored Princess Patricia Priscilla makes her chambermaid
switch identities with her so she can attend the village school, her attitude
changes and she plans a new way to celebrate her sixteenth birthday.
ISBN 978-0-547-23869-2
[1. Princesses—Fiction. 2. Birthdays—Fiction. 3. Schools—
Fiction. 4. Conduct of life—Fiction.] I. Feiffer, Jules, ill.
II. Title.
PZ7.L9673Bi 2010
[Fic]—dc22
2009032966

Manufactured in the United States of America
DOC 10 9 8 7 6 5 4 3 2 1
4500215868

To Will and Sophie Clark,
and the librarians in their lives.

1.

The Princess

When Princess Patricia Priscilla woke on the morning of the day that was five days before her birthday, her first thoughts were not *Oh, I am almost another year older, hardly a child anymore!* or *I wonder what fabulous gifts will be presented to me at the Birthday Ball six nights from now!*

No. Her thoughts were *Bored, bored, bored.*

The princess blinked, then sat up against the seven silk-covered pillows (in seven subtly different shades of royal colors ranging from the palest lavender to the richest purple) that were strewn across the head of her magnificent carved hickory poplar bed.

She snapped her fingers to awaken her yellow long-haired cat, who was still sound asleep near her feet. Delicious opened one amber eye and yawned, showing pointed, highly polished teeth, and then extended four sets of claws in a morning stretch. The cat stabbed at one of the embroidered sunflowers on the elaborate bedcover and pulled one thread loose and then another.

"Please don't be so vicious, Delicious," the princess said in a mildly scolding voice. "It makes me yearn to have a sunflower to tear apart myself. I'm so terribly bored."

The cat looked up and narrowed her eyes to glittery slits. The princess read her mind. She was thinking, in a commanding kind of think: *Feed me.*

"All right," the princess said. She reached for the thick golden bell cord that hung beside the bed, and pulled at it. Then she made an affectionate kissing sound toward her cat and pulled a second, smaller bell cord that dangled beside the first.

Immediately, many levels below in the tall castle, things began to happen.

Three floors down, in the bell room, an antechamber to the basement kitchen of the castle, the two bells rang. One was a dainty brass bell with a pleasant, melodic tinkle, and the other was a small tin one that simply clinked. The bell boy, a young village lad new to the job, was crouched on the floor of the bell room, playing with a shabby set of dominoes. When he heard the small sounds, he looked up at the bell board. He could not read. But beside each bell was a carefully delineated outline.

He saw the small brass bell, which was still vibrating, and beside it the silhouette of a young woman with ringlets and a crown.

"Princess!" he called out, as his job required.

Below it, he looked at the tin bell and its corresponding long-tailed silhouette.

"And cat!" he shouted.

Then he returned to his dominoes, which he was arranging in a line.

In the next room, a chilly stone-floored chamber where food was stored on long tables, an aproned woman with gray disheveled hair was arranging cupcakes in rows.

"Princess and cat!" she called toward the main kitchen.

"Princess, aye!" called three kitchen maids, identical triplets, in three-part harmony. The harmony was not a requirement of their job, but they had

been working on it, hoping to advance in a musical direction that would eventually take them out of the damp, cheerless kitchen. One, the soprano, immediately cracked two eggs into a pan in which butter was already sizzling, on the top of the huge castle stove. Another, a mezzo-soprano, with practiced motion, poured milk into a silver pitcher. The third, the alto, still humming, set a tray on the table and placed on it a small vase holding several flowers picked only minutes before from the castle garden.

"Cat, aye!" grumbled a serving boy. He was elderly, close to eighty. Once he had been a butler, a much more important job, but he had recently been demoted to serving boy (even worse, serving boy in charge of house animals!) after an arthritic hip had caused him to stumble in the dining room and spill hot chocolate on the queen's taffeta skirt. He resented his job and especially his title—serving boy, indeed!—but there was nothing to be done, because he did not wish to retire and stay home with his ill-tempered wife in the small cottage that resounded with her scolds and complaints. He rose with a small groan, holding his hip, from the place he'd been sitting, and shuffled to the side table where two dozen sardines had been laid out on a large tin plate. He peered at them carefully and selected four of the lesser sardines, the ones with the glisten that was not quite as bright (and one with a ragged tear in its tail end), which he placed in the bowl marked DELICIOUS. The other bowls, marked with the names of other housecats, were still empty and waiting, their meals having not yet been summoned.

The elderly serving boy placed the bowl of sardines on the tray just as the soprano maid, with a little trill as she rehearsed some high notes she'd been having trouble with, slid the two cooked eggs onto a plate and set it beside the flower vase and the milk pitcher.

"Pulley Boy!" the serving boy called, and hobbled back to his rocking chair.

The bell boy's older brother rose from the chair where he'd been half dozing, half watching the dominoes, and ran to the kitchen to collect the tray. He had been selected for the job because of his speed. Four village boys had applied. But he was quickest on his feet.

The pulley boy ran, the tray so steady on his

hands that not a drop of milk appeared over the lip of the little pitcher, into the long hall lined with seventeen square wooden doors, each painted with a silhouette just above its latch. Because he was accustomed to his job, the pulley boy no longer had to examine the silhouettes. He went immediately to the door designated for the princess's bedchamber. He lifted the latch, opened the door, placed the tray onto the wooden shelf suspended within, and pulled the thick rope, which lifted it three floors above so quickly that the eggs did not cool.

"Princess and cat aloft!" he called loudly while the tray rose through the thick walls.

"Princess and cat aloft, aye," the entire population of the castle kitchen murmured, heads nodding, and went back to their work. The pulley boy settled again in his chair. His younger brother, the bell boy, set the last domino carefully on edge, then tapped it and watched the line collapse. He clapped his hands in delight. At the same time, he remained alert, listening, waiting for the next bell to ring, for that was his job.

Above, in the bedchamber of Princess Patricia Priscilla, a young chambermaid with freckles took the breakfast tray from its wall opening and placed it on a small round table by the window. She salted the eggs, poured the milk into a pewter goblet, and set the cat's bowl of sardines on the floor beneath the tablecloth. The cat, who always breakfasted at the princess's feet, leapt from the bed, ran to the bowl, and sniffed.

"It's nutritious, Delicious," the princess told her pet. She said that every morning. It amused her.

"Happy Monday-before-your-birthday, Princess Patricia Priscilla," the chambermaid murmured. She held out a silk dressing gown. The princess slipped her arms into its sleeves and sat down at the table.

"Thank you," the princess replied politely. She picked up a fork, took a small bite of her breakfast, and gazed through the window to the land below and around the castle. It was a beautiful day. The sky was cloudless and clear blue, and below, the farmland stretched in rounded hills of green and gold, each field outlined by darker green rows of hedge. She could see some cows, spotted black and white, grazing, and on the smooth dirt path some small children played, rolling a large blue and white striped ball and laughing. The air was so clear that the sound of their laughter rose to her window almost like notes of a song.

Another day was beginning. Princess Patricia Priscilla sighed. "I'm so very bored," she said.

2.

The Schoolmaster

*B*elow, in the village, the new young schoolmaster was preparing his classroom. He set the little desks in straight rows, looked at the alignment, thought, then shook his head and moved the desks again until they formed a semicircle facing his own, larger desk. He decided that he liked it better that way.

His name was Rafe. Villagers, peasants that they were, all had short names. It distinguished them from nobility and royalty. Earls, dukes, counts, lords, ladies, and princesses could have names as long as they wished, even adding additional names as they chose, although sometimes the lengthy additions became unwieldy and hard to remember.

There had been an incident once when the queen had arranged a ceremony to bestow special honors on a knight who had done a chivalrous deed.

"Arise!" the queen had called out, for he was on his knees before her and she had tapped his shoulder with her jeweled scepter and lowered around his neck a decorative ribbon from which dangled a medal. "Arise, Sir . . ."

But there had followed an embarrassing hesitation. His name was Mortimer, and she remembered that, for she had known this knight for years. But in recent months he had taken additional names, designating himself "the Manly" and "the Magnificent" and "Most Masculine." The queen simply drew a blank. She stared at him and he stared back, lifting his head slightly from its bowed position, but it would have been unseemly for him to speak during the solemn ceremony, and in any case he was puzzled by her hesitation, not realizing what it meant.

The king, who had been watching from his throne next to the queen's, whispered to his wife.

"Sir Mortimer the Manly, the Magnificent, Most Masculine," the king whispered in a very low voice. But he knew it was useless. The queen was quite hard of hearing. Both of her ears had been frostbitten during a Winter Carnival when she had, as a young woman, been too vain to wear her fur hat, and her hearing had been much diminished ever since. She did not hear her husband's helpful whisper at all.

But the queen had much presence of mind, which very often compensated for the things she lacked, such as perfect hearing. On this occasion she simply stood in a regal fashion and announced to the assembled nobility: "Let us all together *intone* the name of our newly honored knight. Ready?" She held up her scepter.

"Sir . . ." she began, and then looked at the gathering expectantly.

The king had a large baritone voice. "Sir Mortimer . . ." he intoned.

Finally the entire audience, which was made up of forty earls, twenty-two dukes, many spouses and concubines, three buffoons, and a barrister, perceived what was expected of them.

"Sir Mortimer the Manly, the Magnificent, Most Masculine!" they intoned, and the knight arose.

No such problem ever took place among the peasant populace. Their names, like that of the young schoolmaster, were short and easy to say. Nell. Jack. Will.

In fact, those were the very names that the schoolmaster, Rafe, on this day when school was soon to begin, wrote on small cards in his best calligraphy, along with the names of the other children who would be his pupils:

Nell

Jack

Will

Fred

Liz

Mick

Beth

Anne

Kate

Ben

He placed each card upon one of the wooden desks. Then he fed the small hedgehog that was caged in the corner. He had brought it to be the class pet and to teach the children responsibility for creatures.

He placed the large orange dunce cap in a highly visible spot in order to discourage misbehavior.

Rafe remembered from his own childhood and school days how humiliating it was to wear the dunce cap. Though he had always been a good student, diligent at his lessons, from time to time he had indulged his own sense of fun in ways that the stern schoolmaster, Herr Gutmann, had disapproved of. As punishment he had been ordered to don the humiliating orange cap and stand in front of the class.

Now, Rafe supposed, as schoolmaster himself, he would have to punish misconduct. He dreaded the moment when he would be forced to place the dunce cap on the head of one of the fun-loving children who were to be his pupils.

He could hear them outside, the village children, playing with a ball in the path. Soon it would be time for school to begin. He was a little nervous now, on his first day at the job. He had studied Teaching Methods at the academy, and he had done well there, excelling at Inscribing and Declaiming. He considered himself very good at Games of the

Imagination and moderately adept at Proverbs. But his Mathematical Calculations were a little weak, he knew, and he was very lacking in Stern Demeanor.

"You must try to curb your affability," the Teaching Methods professor had said at his evaluation. "Work at being stern."

"I do try," Rafe said.

"Your face makes it difficult, I know," the professor said sympathetically.

"My face?"

No one had ever commented on Rafe's face before, except his mother. He remembered dimly that she had always called him the bonniest of her boys, a sweet little joke between them because he was her only son.

His face was actually fairly ordinary. His bright brown eyes were flecked with yellow, and he had a high forehead onto which his brown hair often fell, though he brushed it back so frequently with his hand that it had become a habit.

"A stern face," the professor explained, "requires that the mouth be set in a line. Like so." He demonstrated, setting his mouth by pulling it tightly against his teeth. He looked quite fierce, actually, when he did it, and Rafe was a little unnerved.

"And the forehead should be furrowed," the professor went on. "With the forehead furrowed, the eyebrows quite naturally fall into a state of increased bushiness. Like so."

He demonstrated again, this time setting his

mouth and at the same time furrowing his forehead.

"It's an extremely stern look," Rafe agreed, feeling quite uncomfortable at the sight of it.

"Yes. Well. Work at it."

"Yes, sir."

"Your face falls into affable lines. The corners of
your mouth turn up. Not good for a schoolmaster.
It deceives the children."

"Oh, I certainly don't want to be guilty of de-
ceiving the children!" Rafe had said. It was something he felt most strongly about.

Now it was his first day as
schoolmaster, a day that had
come upon him sooner than he
had expected, because of the
sudden retirement of the previous teacher, who had held the
job for many years. Arranging
his classroom, Rafe tried also to
arrange his face. He furrowed
his brow and set his mouth in a
line. It was hard to hold it that
way, because it ached a little, and

though he didn't realize it, the corners of his mouth kept creeping out into the beginning of a smile.

Herr Gutmann, Rafe's own teacher from his childhood, had been gray-haired and bearded. Rafe, in contrast, was quite young—only eighteen. He had completed his studies and had been preparing for an apprenticeship in a distant domain when quite suddenly he had been called back to this village, the very one in which he had been born, because of the sudden departure of Herr Gutmann.

(He had not been told why Herr Gutmann had left. But it was rumored that the love of his life, a woman named Gertrude, had been widowed and had sent an imploring letter from the distant domain where she lived, saying she was now lonely.)

Thinking of it, Rafe wondered what it might be like to have a love of one's life. It had never happened to him. What was love, anyway? He wasn't certain. He thought of the females he knew well.

His mother? Oh, yes! He had loved her. He remembered her singing him to sleep when he was small. But she had died not long after giving birth to his little sister, when he was still a tiny boy. She was buried now in the churchyard down the lane from the schoolhouse. He had tipped his hat in her honor as he had walked past this very morning.

His sister? He had loved her, too. But sadly she also was lost to him forever. She had simply disappeared while he was away pursuing his studies. When Rafe, on returning from the teachers' academy, had asked his father about the whereabouts of his sister, the burly, loud-voiced man had wiped some breakfast grease off his beard with one hand and bellowed, "Useless things, girls! I sold her!" and would give no further explanation. So he had mourned his beloved younger sister ever since, and without even a grave toward which he could tip his hat.

Other females? Well. He had a cousin. But she was a dull girl who tended to talk too much, and aimlessly, telling long, tedious stories with no point to them.

Then there was Aunt Chloë, who worked as the cook at the castle. But she had whiskers and warts. Rafe knew that beauty was within. But when the *without* had whiskers and warts, it was hard to venture beyond.

Anyway, none of those, he thought, had anything to do with the love of one's life. It was a concept he would probably never understand. Rafe
sighed and stopped thinking about love and what it
might mean, realizing that it would probably never
come to him. He would love teaching and would
love his pupils; perhaps that would be enough.
Carefully he stacked his papers on his desk in a
tidy pile. He cleaned his fingernails one more time
with a small knife that he kept in his pocket. Then
he took out his handkerchief and wiped the dust
once again from his shoes.

I will do my best to be a good teacher.

He said it to himself two more times.

I will do my best to be a good teacher.

I will do my best to be a good teacher.

Then he looked at the carved cuckoo clock on
the classroom wall. (It had been his mother's, but
he didn't want to think about that. It made him
sad.) The clock told him that it was time. He took
a deep breath and went to the doorway to ring the
bell that summoned the village children to school.

3.
The Chambermaid

"I don't see how you can be bored, miss, when you got so many lovely things."

Princess Patricia Priscilla frowned. "Nothing I want," she said to the chambermaid.

The freckle-faced girl picked up a silver-backed hairbrush. For a moment she looked at her own face reflected in the silver. She grinned at herself, and blushed.

"Not this, miss?" She held up the brush. "It's beautiful. If you like, I can brush your hair for you, a hundred strokes. I can count to one hundred, truly I can. And you can sit at the mirror and watch yourself while I do it."

The princess sighed. "We do that every day. I'm

tired of it. I know! What if . . ." Her face lit up with interest.

"What, miss?"

"What if we turned things around and I brushed *your* hair a hundred strokes?" Princess Patricia Priscilla reached for the hairbrush.

But the chambermaid hastily returned it to the dressing table and backed away. "Oh, no, miss. That wouldn't do."

"Not allowed?"

"Not allowed at all."

"Punishable by torture?"

"Oh, I dunno. Maybe not torture, not for that. But punishment, for sure!"

The chambermaid paled and looked so genuinely alarmed that the princess sighed and gave up the idea. She picked up the brush and pulled it through her own hair a few times. "There," she said, with a sigh. "Now I should dress, I suppose. Have you chosen a frock for me for today?"

"I thought the blue organdy, miss? It matches your eyes."

Princess Patricia Priscilla groaned. "It scratches," she said, "and causes a rash on my shoulders."

"Then the yellow silk? It falls all smooth and soft."

Princess Patricia Priscilla made a face. "My cat slides off my lap when I wear silk," she pointed out, and then looked affectionately at her pet. "The yellow silk is inauspicious, isn't it, Delicious?" The cat yawned and tidily cleaned her whiskers.

The princess wandered to the window and looked down at the village again. The children were still playing in the path near the schoolhouse. She could hear their laughter.

"What is your name?" she asked suddenly, turning back to the chambermaid.

"Seventeenth chambermaid, miss." The girl curtsied.

"No, no—I mean your *real* name."

A blush darkened the chambermaid's freckled face. "Tess," she whispered.

"And you're a peasant girl, right? From the village?"

"Yes, miss. Born there."

"Did you play on that path?" The princess pointed through the window.

The chambermaid went to the window and

looked down. She nodded. "Yes, miss," she whispered.

"And went to that school?"

"Till I was thirteen. Last year, that was."

"You're only fourteen? You're as tall as I am, and I'll be sixteen next Saturday."

"Yes, miss. I'm a great galoomph of a girl. My pa said I was tall as a tree, and should be cut off at the knees." The girl stood awkwardly, trying to shrink herself.

"Don't do that. Stand up straight and tall. That is a command."

"Yes, miss." The girl straightened her shoulders and bobbed in a curtsy once again.

"Stop that bobbing up and down. It makes me dizzy to watch it. I want you to tell me about your life, Tess."

"My life? But I haven't even got one yet!"

"Of course you do. Everyone does. Where were you born? Look down through the window. Can you see your house? Or I suppose it is called a hut, or a hovel?"

The chambermaid peered down. "Over there," she said, after she figured it out. She gestured. "Past the schoolhouse, past the graveyard, through them trees. You can see only the thatch of the roof from here. I was born in that very cottage.

"We call it a cottage, miss," she explained apologetically.

"Cottage, then. So you were born right there, and you have a father, I know, because you mentioned him—"

"Pa," the chambermaid said in a small voice.

"And a mother? A ma, I suppose you'd call her?"

"Died," whispered the girl.

"Oh, pity. But I suppose you go back to visit your pa? Do you have days off from the castle?"

"I got my free day every second Tuesday. But I don't go back. Pa never wants to see me again. He said that." The girl lowered her head and sniffed.

"Oh, dear. I do hope you are not going to whimper. My head aches when people whimper."

"No, miss. I won't." The chambermaid bit her lip.

The princess picked up the hairbrush and began to brush her own hair again, absentmindedly. "So you were born right there and lived there for thirteen years, and went to school—"

"I did love school, miss."

"—and then you applied for the castle job—"

"My ma's brother's widow works in the castle kitchen, and recommended me."

"—and you left school, and your parents—"

"My ma was dead. Withered away when I was born."

"Oh, yes, sorry. I forgot that. Your mother died. Pity. And your pa said he never wanted to see you again and your knees should be cut off—"

"No. My legs. At the knees. 'Cuz I was a great galoomph and he didn't want me around."

"So you left school, and—"

"I was doing fine," the girl said earnestly. "Not like some. Knew all my letters and numbers. Could read good. And knew music, too! The schoolmaster said I sang like a lark."

"A lark? Indeed! And do you sing, still?"

"Only down in the kitchen. Not allowed anywheres else in the castle."

The princess set down the hairbrush and took off her dressing gown. She opened the door of the large wardrobe to examine the long rows of frocks and gowns in many colors and fabrics. She frowned in indecision.

"In the kitchen," the chambermaid went on, her excitement increasing in the telling, "we *all* sing! The three serving girls, they can sing in *parts!* They practice all the time. And sometimes Cook, she beats time with a wooden spoon, and even the serving boy, though he's old and has false teeth that whistle, even he comes in on the choruses and the *tra-la*s. And the pulley boy!" The chambermaid closed her eyes and sighed.

"Pulley boy?" The princess turned from the wardrobe.

"Yes, miss. Him that pulls the food up from the kitchen. He's the fastest boy on his feet! And steady! Never a drop spilt! He can't read, but he sings like an angel," the chambermaid added, blushing, "and he's handsome, too."

Princess Patricia Priscilla began to laugh. "I expect I'll be hearing more about the pulley boy. But not now."

"No, miss, now you must dress." The chambermaid reassumed her attentive attitude. "Have you decided what gown?"

"I have. And now I am going to give you a command."

"Yes, miss?"

"And what must you do when given a command?"

"Obey. And curtsy first."

"Even if it is an odd command?"

"Yes, miss, I suppose so." The chambermaid looked a little uncertain.

"Tess," commanded the princess, "take off your clothes."

4.
The Disguise

"Miss! I couldn't!"

"Don't be silly. Of course you can. First the apron. I want to see what dress you wear beneath the apron."

Nervously the chambermaid untied the sash of her starched white pinafore and let the wide apron fall loose. She pulled her arms free from the ruffled shoulders, folded the apron, and laid it on a pink damask chair.

"It's quite ordinary, isn't it? The dress, I mean." The princess examined it and felt the homespun brown fabric between her thumb and forefinger.

"I think it's nice." The chambermaid spoke a

little defensively. "I never had one so nice till I come here to work."

"Of course it's nice. I simply meant that it is quite ordinary compared to the satins and organdies I have to wear every day. Tell me something, Tess. Would this be the kind of dress a village girl might wear to school?"

Tess wrinkled her face, thinking about it. "Aye," she said, "I guess. Maybe more raggedy and patched, for most. And not with shoes." She looked down at her own feet, shod in sturdy buckled leather over thick black stockings.

"No shoes?"

"No, miss. Not in this weather, at least. In winter, when it's cold, maybe clogs. But these"— she pointed to her feet with a certain amount of pride—"these here are castle shoes."

"Well, you keep those on, then. And your underclothes. But give me your dress."

"My dress? Why?"

"It is a command."

Tess sighed, curtsied, and began to unbutton the simple brown dress.

∽⌒∾

"There, now! Tell me what you think. Do I look like a simple village girl?"

Princess Patricia Priscilla stood back and posed against the embroidered draperies that framed the large double window. She was wearing the homely dress and her feet were bare.

The chambermaid, wearing her muslin under-shift, her bony shoulders and arms exposed, looked critically at her. "Hair too fancy. Feet too clean," she said, after a moment.

"I was afraid of that."

"I could fix the hair, I guess."

"Do so, then."

The chambermaid mussed the princess's long curls and then braided the hair into two uneven pigtails.

"Shall you put a ribbon at each end?" the princess asked.

"Oh my, no. That would be princesslike. Here's how we do." The chambermaid removed the sprigs of flowers from the crystal vase on the breakfast tray. Deftly she tied the ends of the braids with twisted flower stems.

"Oh, I think I look wonderfully rustic and primitive!" said the princess, standing before the long

looking glass. "I'll dirty my feet when I am out-doors."

The chambermaid, standing beside her, staring at her own reflected image, groaned. "Blimey, I look bare-naked! I'm downright humiliated."

"Here." The princess handed Tess the dressing gown that was draped on the bed. "Put this on and wear it till I return."

"I can't, miss! They'd see, and I'd be punished!"

"No. No one will see you. You stay right in my room and I will leave instructions that no one is to enter.

"Look over there, Tess, at the bookshelves! Filled with books. You said you could read. You may read any book you want. That will pass the time while I'm gone."

The little freckled chambermaid stared in rap-ture at the crowded shelves. "Lordy," she breathed. "I hope my ma is looking down and can see this. Me in silk, with books!"

5.

The Escape

$\mathscr{P}$rincess Patricia Priscilla, her homespun dress hidden under a cloak, made her way down the castle stairs, followed by Delicious, twitching her thick tail. She knew that she would not encounter her father. An old nursery rhyme contained great truth: *The king was in his counting house . . .*

The princess's father, King Lepidoptera, spent most of his time in his counting house, which was a separate small building to the left of the west tower. He was not there to "count out his money," as the rhyme described, because a team of exchequers worked continuously on that task in a vast room called the vault, which was in a secret location. There was a great deal of money, more coming in all the time—taxes and tributes and tithes—and fourteen highly intelligent money managers counted and sorted it twenty-four hours a day, making lists and notes and calculations with quill pens.

The counting house was different. In it the king kept his vast collections of butterflies. He acquired them, sorted them, organized them, and labeled them. He had old shelves and drawers removed and new shelves and drawers installed. A team of skilled carpenters worked on nothing but the king's collection cabinetry, though from time to time one carpenter might be summoned to the castle briefly to repair a wobbly chair or a creaking floorboard.

Because she knew that her father went to his counting house each morning, the princess was not worried about encountering him as she tiptoed stealthily down the wide stone stairs. The stone was chilly on her bare feet. Ordinarily her feet were unclothed only when she bathed, and then only very briefly and under the warmest of circumstances.

But she liked the feeling of touching something true, like stone. "I wonder what *dirt* will feel like," she said softly, even though no one was nearby.

Tess the chambermaid had been left behind in the bedchamber, curled up with *Alice in Wonderland*, murmuring "Blimey!" each time an amazing thing happened, which was every other paragraph.

"I'm going now, Tess," the princess had announced. "I'm going to do just what you suggested, and tell the schoolmaster I am new to the village."

"Blimey," Tess said, barely looking up. "Now she's got herself a cake that says 'Eat me'! And what happened to that rabbit, I ask you!"

"I command you to listen for a moment."

The chambermaid carefully marked her place with a finger, and looked up.

"'My father is dead and my ma a poor widow newly come to the village who does washing for lazy folk.' I'll tell him that."

"Say *Pa*, not *Father*."

"Yes, of course. I almost forgot. 'My pa is dead, killed by—let me think—a wild boar.'"

The chambermaid nodded. Her glance slid to the page.

"And you promise that he'll take me as a pupil, and give me a desk."

"Uh-huh."

The princess glared at her.

"I mean, 'Yes, miss.'"

"Oh, dear, I hope I'm not forgetting anything important. I'll smear my feet with dirt on the path so they'll look like true peasant feet, humble and smudged. Are you certain it's all right if my cat comes with me?"

The chambermaid shrugged. "Cats is everywhere. Nobody notices cats."

"I'm so very excited."

The chambermaid nodded and turned her eyes to the book again.

"Aren't you excited, also, at such an adventure?"

"Yes, miss. Excited."

The princess turned to leave.

"Blimey," said the chambermaid, absorbed in the book, examining a drawing of Alice, "now she's gone and grown *huge*."

Although her father was, as she had predicted, in the counting house, the princess did encounter her mother, the queen, as she tried to creep away unnoticed. Queen Romelda Rebozo emerged from her private beauty salon on the second landing just as the princess was tiptoeing past.

"Good Lord Almighty, what on earth have you done to your hair?" the queen bellowed.

She always bellowed. It was because she was so deaf.

The princess reached up and touched the end of one untidy pigtail.

"It's the latest style," she explained to her mother. "It's rustic."

"Plastic? It certainly is not. Your father outlawed plastic years ago." The queen noticed the bare feet next, though the princess tried to crouch and cover them with her gathered skirt.

"Oh, I see, you're going bathing. That's why your hair is done up so oddly. But you should wear your bathing slippers, Patricia Priscilla. Don't catch a chill. Five days until the ball! We need you healthy! You know what happens at the ball?"

She waited.

"I said: *You know what happens at the ball?*"

The princess hadn't realized it was a question. "Music," she replied to her mother.

"Eh?" The queen cupped her hand behind her ear. "Who's sick, did you say? No one is sick. What a foolish thing to say!"

"I said *music!*" the princess shouted.

"Indeed! Full orchestra." The queen beamed. "Extra violins! And a dwarf who plays the bassoon. What else?"

"Banquet food," the princess said.

"Eh? Bank a few? What a foolish—"

"*Banquet food!*" the princess said again, more loudly.

"Oh, right! Creamed pigeons, to start. Truffles and roast goat, salmon timbale, braised asparagus with pistachios, pickled turnips, artichokes stuffed with goose liver, pheasant breast *en croute*—"

"Mother, I have to go. My toes are freezing!" The princess descended a few steps.

"What was that? Toast is easy? Who said it

wasn't? We're not having toast! What a foolish thing to say!" The queen tsk-tsked.

"And also," she went on, "don't forget the most important thing!"

The princess, at the foot of the stairs now, looked back. Her mother beamed down at her.

"What's that, Mother?"

"Eh?"

"What's the most important thing?"

"Suitors!" the queen bellowed. "You'll be sixteen! Marriageable! It's time for suitors!"

The princess scurried along, avoiding housemaids and polishing boys busy at their never-ending scrubbing and wiping and shining. She tried to put her mother's final word out of her mind. *Suitors!* The princess hated the thought of it.

In the huge entry hall of the castle, she hung her cloak on an iron hook near a mounted stag's head. Then she pulled open the heavy carved oak door and went outside. Behind her, Delicious, the cat, slid out just before the massive door closed on her thick, yellow, very sensitive tail.

It was not that the princess had never been outside before. On the contrary, as a younger child
she had often been taken out for an airing by her
nursemaid, and the two of them had skipped and
hopped, laughing, on the finely mowed lawn beside
the flower gardens. Now that she was older, the
princess had often attended fetes and celebrations,
sometimes at great distances to which she had
traveled by the castle coach and its four magnificent sleek brown horses, who were decorated with
plumes that bobbed with their heads. Sometimes,
too, she had paid solicitous visits to the poor and
downtrodden, accompanying her mother, the two
of them followed by servants carrying baskets of
nicely wrapped food and herbal medications.

But this was different. Now she was barefoot,
clothed only in an extremely humble frock. Now
she was alone except for her thoughts—*Suitors!* she
said to herself again, with a shudder—and her pet.

"Listen, Delicious!" The two of them, princess
and cat, cocked their heads and stood motionless,
listening to the sound of the many birds that twit-
tered and chirped in the trees. The cat's ears
twitched. A small pink tongue emerged and licked

thin cat lips. The cat's tail moved slowly back and forth.

"Don't be silly," the princess said, scolding her pet affectionately. "Peasant cats eat birds, of course, because they are poor and hungry and have no choice. But you are a castle cat with sardines at your beck and call. Stop looking avaricious, Delicious."

The cat, knowing the princess was correct, was embarrassed, and stilled her twitching tail.

The pair strode quickly down the well-kept path that led to the castle entrance. In the distance, across the vast lawn, gardeners were trimming hedges and watering a bed of peonies. No one noticed the princess as she pushed open the scrolled iron gate and left the castle grounds.

Outside, the path was no longer raked and neatly tended. Thick with dust and pebbles, it curved through the trees, and they followed it until the castle gate was out of sight behind them. Here the princess knelt and rubbed dirt onto her feet.

"Look, now my fingernails are dirty, too!" she said, speaking to the cat as she often did, since she usually had no one else. "I wonder if poor peasants have dirty fingernails. I suppose they do. And faces? Here, I'll smear some dirt across my cheek."

She did so while the cat watched.

"Now I am perfectly disguised as a pitiful peasant," the princess said with satisfaction. "Come along quickly. I don't hear the children playing anymore, and I think they must have gone into the school. So we should hurry. And no need, incidentally, to be surreptitious, Delicious. We blend in nicely."

The cat followed her compliantly, though her attention was diverted now and then by things that rustled the bushes and tall grass bordering the path. Mice. Chipmunks. A toad. A small green snake. Delicious yearned to prowl and pounce.

"Isn't this fun?" the princess said as they made their way hastily along the path toward the little school. "I am not one bit bored!"

6.
The Schoolhouse

"I'm a poor peasant girl only recently come to live in the village because my mother was killed by a wild boar and my pa has to take in washing."

The princess stood nervously in the doorway of the schoolhouse. She looked down at her own dirty bare toes, then, because of the silence, back up at the face of the schoolmaster. His mouth was set in a line and his forehead was furrowed. He looked very stern, just as Tess, the chambermaid, had described.

The children, each one seated at a small desk, giggled.

I said it wrong, she thought. "I mean my pa was

killed, that's what, and it's my mother that has to take in washing. I mean my ma."

"And you would like to become a pupil?"

"Yes."

"Yes what?"

"Yes, ah, I would like to."

He frowned and his forehead furrowed further.

"*Yes, sir* is the response," he said sternly.

The princess had never said "Yes, sir" to anyone in her life. But now she imitated the chambermaid, bobbed in a curtsy, and murmured, "Yes, sir."

"You're quite tall for a schoolgirl."

What was the phrase the chambermaid had used? "I'm a great galoomph of a girl."

The schoolmaster winced visibly at the phrase. "Please don't refer to yourself in that demeaning way," he said abruptly. Then his voice softened. "You are tall and slender as a young willow tree, supple and lovely. Remember that."

She nodded. "Yes, sir. Young willow tree."

The schoolmaster looked around the room, and his gaze settled on one pudgy boy. "Fred," he said, and beckoned to the boy.

"Yes, sir?"

"Move that empty desk, the one in the corner,

and place it at the girls' end of our semicircle."

The boy obeyed and began to drag the desk to its place.

"And I," the schoolmaster said, "will make a nametag for your desk. That is, if you will tell me your name, which you have so far neglected to do."

"Blimey," the princess said aloud, imitating the chambermaid again. "I forgot."

"Excuse me?" The schoolmaster was at his tall desk, holding his quill pen.

"I forgot I had to have a name."

He eyed her curiously.

She cleared her throat. "Ah, it's Pat," she said. "Quite a short name because I'm merely a humble peasant."

"Well, that wasn't so hard, was it, to remember your own name?" He began to write the letters.

"No."

He looked up. "No what?"

"No, it wasn't. I mean: No, sir."

For the first time the schoolmaster smiled slightly. Then he placed the nametag, with its carefully lettered

Pat

on her desk. He gestured to her to take her seat.

When she was seated, he leaned forward and looked at her more closely. He sighed. "Your face is dirty," he observed, "and so are your fingernails."

"Because I'm a poor peasant," the princess replied.

"Everyone in this room is a poor peasant," he said sternly, "including me. But we are all clean."

The princess looked around and saw that it was true. How had she gotten things so wrong? The other pupils' feet were dirty, all of them bare and coated with dust from the path (the schoolmaster wore high-topped suede shoes), but their faces were scrubbed, their hair was brushed, and their fingernails were clean.

"Go outside to the pump and wash," he told her. "Then come back quietly and take your seat for a spelling lesson.

"And," he added, "when you return, leave your cat outside."

The cat had curled around her feet, under the desk. Now opening both amber eyes at the sound of the word "cat," Delicious yawned, stood, and followed the princess as she left the room.

"You stay out here and lie in the sun," she told

her pet as she dutifully cleaned her hands and face at the pump. "Wait for me. At the end of the school day, we'll go back to the castle and I'll summon your nice sardines for supper." She stroked the furry neck briefly.

The banished cat yawned and looked around, then extended the claws of all four feet, trying them out, because they had never been used for anything beyond dismantling embroidery. Now, above, a nest of plump and tasty-looking baby wrens was clearly visible. Across the schoolyard the cat perceived an appetizing small rodent of some sort, nibbling on a fern. The tip of a rough, pink, glistening tongue emerged.

The princess could almost read her cat's mind. "Don't be malicious, Delicious," she commanded, and shook her finger in warning. Then she left the cat there and returned, scrubbed clean, to the schoolroom.

"Oh, it was lovely, Tess, just lovely," the princess said at the end of the day, back in her bedchamber. "We had poetry and penmanship, and in geography I learned the names of all the domains, in alphabetical order."

"Domains, miss?" The chambermaid, reclothed, finished buttoning her dress and reached for the starched apron that had lain all day folded on the damask chair.

"You know, other principalities and kingdoms. Fiefdoms, too. Places ruled by other royalty, not us."

"Didn't even know there *was* other, miss."

"Oh, of course, there are tons! There's Analgesia, Bulimia, Coagulatia . . ." She sat, then held out her left foot so that the chambermaid could lace and tie her shoe. "I'm reciting them alphabetically," she explained. "Dyspepsia," she said next.

"I heard about that one," the chambermaid said. "There's a duke there."

The princess made a face of disgust. "Duke Desmond. A face like a warthog. No other domain has a ruler so hideous."

"Sorry to hear that, miss. There, this foot's done. Hold out the other."

The princess did so. "Why are you sorry to hear about stupid old Duke Desmond? He never comes here."

"Oh, but he will, ma'am. His name is on the list."

"What list? Is there a list of repulsive rulers?" The princess laughed, then reached for her hair-brush.

The chambermaid bit her lip uneasily. "Maybe I shouldn't have said, miss. But there's a list in the kitchen so's Cook can plan the food. A list of who's coming to your Birthday Ball."

Angrily the princess flung the silver-backed brush to her bed. Her cat, lying there, looked up, startled.

"Oh, don't be so suspicious, Delicious," the princess said in an irritated voice. "I wasn't aiming at you.

"Why would that warthog be invited to my ball?"

The chambermaid looked very nervous. She curtsied and began to edge herself toward the door.

"You know something I don't know! Tell me at once! This is a command!"

The chambermaid curtsied again and whispered it. "He's a suitor, miss. He's on the suitor list."

"No!" The princess gasped in horror.

"Yes, miss."

"Are there others? Who else is on the list?"

"I need a minute to think, miss." The chamber-maid closed her eyes and tried to see the list in her mind. "Duke Desmond of Dyspepsia."

"You said that already. The warthog. Who else?"

"Ah, Prince Percival of—"

"Oh, no!" the princess wailed. "Of Pustula! Not *him!* He has dandruff, and he oozes foul-smelling hair oil!" She flung herself onto her bed. The cat hopped down in dismay and moved to the window seat instead.

"Anyone else?" the princess asked with a groan.

"Just one, miss. It's an odd one, though. Because it says two names together. Let me think."

"You don't need to. Two names together means only one thing." The princess was speaking now in a resigned voice, as if she had no more groans or wails left. "It's the Lords Colin and Cuthbert the Conjoint, isn't it?"

"Yes, miss, that's it."

"I knew it! My mother finds them fascinating because they're attached together. But they're *coarse* and *rude.* They bicker continuously, and they belch, too, and reek! They never bathe because no tub fits them both at once."

"Miss," the chambermaid asked timidly, "may I go, please? It's close to suppertime and I want to be there to watch the pulley boy."

"The pulley boy. I suppose he's on *your* list of suitors?"

"Oh, no, miss!"

"Only joking. Go on. I'll see you in the morning. Be here early. I was late for school today. I want to arrive on time tomorrow."

"Miss!" The chambermaid looked surprised. "You're going back?"

The princess propped herself up against the pillows. "Of course I am. My first day as a peasant was the loveliest day I've ever had. I was not bored for a minute."

"The schoolmaster's stern, though," the chambermaid pointed out.

"A little. But handsome."

The chambermaid wrinkled her face. "*Handsome?* No, miss. He ain't, not at all. He has a very fierce face."

"Perhaps. But it appealed to me. Do you know his name, Tess? I asked him but he said we should all just call him Schoolmaster."

Tess nodded. "It's a foreign name. *Herr Gutmann.* He's from far away. They say he come from a noble family."

"That's odd," said the princess. "He said he was a peasant."

"Not him, miss. Maybe he likes to pretend it."

"He *did* wear shoes, now that I think about it."

"Please, miss? It's time for me to go below-stairs."

The princess laughed. "To see your pulley boy. All right, Tess. Run along."

Tess closed the door to the bedchamber behind her. Through it, she heard the princess mutter, "Suitors, schmooters."

7.

The Duke

A warthog has large upcurled tusks, and Duke Desmond, being human, had none. He did, however, have huge, crooked, brown-spotted teeth, and a tuft of coarse copper-colored hair; the two features combined to make him resemble such an animal, so the princess was not inaccurate in her description.

That his disposition was terrible was not surprising. In his defense, it must be said that any human who resembles a warthog is bound to be irritable and testy. His own parents had found it distasteful to look at Desmond when he was young, and when he was a child no other children had

ever invited him to play. Such slights do affect one's personality.

But Duke Desmond did have one attribute. He was immensely wealthy.

Both of his parents had by now passed away, and Duke Desmond ruled the opulent principality of Dyspepsia and owned all of its wealth: oil wells, gold mines, and huge vineyards. The income from all of these came to Desmond. He spent it and spent it on clothes and playthings and trinkets and baubles, but it continued to come. And with the money and the title came power. He was a very powerful man.

Such was his power that he had found a way to forget his own appearance. He had abolished not only all mirrors and looking glasses from Dyspepsia, but also any shiny object that might throw back a reflection. When he traveled, he did so accompanied by bodyguards and courtiers, some of whom went ahead to be certain that all such reflectors were removed from his presence.

So Duke Desmond had found a way to forget what he looked like. He had begun to think of his appearance as pleasing, and the servants he hired had been trained to address him as they might address a handsome man.

"How fine you look this morning, sir!" his manservant would proclaim upon drawing open the curtains of the sleeping chamber each day. Duke Desmond would yawn and stretch and then appear to smile. He never really smiled, but his huge protruding teeth made it impossible for him to close his lips.

Years before, a previous manservant had foolishly suggested to the duke that he brush his teeth, but that unfortunate servant had been confined in the dungeon ever since. By now the teeth were mottled with decay and encrusted with plaque. Perpetual toothache was a further reason for the duke's bad disposition.

No one dared suggest, either, that he comb his hair. Or cut it. The coarse red-brown tuft at the top of his head was long and snarled. When he tossed his head, as he frequently did in fits of anger, the hair moved like a thick whip from side to side, and those in its path were in danger from it. One small serving maid had been knocked to the floor by the hair and had her brain permanently addled. The duke's barrister had made a gift to the maid's family of a large sum of money to make up for it, and other servants had learned to stand clear in the future.

The most heinous of individuals (and Duke Desmond was certainly one of those) all seem to have a deeply hidden sorrow. For the duke, it was that he had no child.

Without a child, he had no heir. When he died, Duke Desmond knew, his wealth—his wells and mines and vineyards—would all go to the populace. *Peasants* would own it all, control it all, and the thought made him seethe with angry despair.

But that was not the whole of it. He wanted a child for another deeply human reason. He wanted someone to love him.

And so he needed a wife.

He had chosen Princess Patricia Priscilla.

It can be said, and *has* been said, often, that money cannot buy happiness. But Duke Desmond thought that it could, and that he had figured out the way to bring it about.

His spies had been sent to the domain where the princess lived with her parents in the castle. They went disguised as peddlers, carrying displays of hair products and encyclopedias. The queen, who began each day with a visit to her private beauty salon, welcomed the spy who proclaimed that he carried a line of amazing shampoos and curling lotions newly invented by cloistered nuns in a distant and holy place.

"Eh?" the queen said to the imposter peddler. "Blistered buns, you say?"

"No, ma'am, *cloistered nuns!*"

"Holstered guns!" she said. "Amazing. I'll take three hundred of each."

The king summoned the other spy to the counting house. He examined the encyclopedia and ordered several to be delivered to the royal library. The imposter peddler wrote down the order meticulously, but in truth his interest was not on the order but on what about the encyclopedia had most interested the king.

It was Volume B.

It was, specifically, butterflies.

Of course the spy had noticed the elaborate shelves that housed the king's butterfly collection and where the mounted winged creatures were on display, with special lighting. They were arranged two ways: one by color, so that the lengthy shelf began with pale yellow and made its way through each gradation and hue—oranges, reds, blues, greens—so that the wall seemed a rainbow. But the opposite wall held the same collection, duplicates, arranged by scientific names: In the section marked NYMPKINGIDAE, the spy saw the amazing

multicolored *Prepona praeneste praenestina;* nearby, under ORNITHOPTERA, was the semitranslucent *Papuana;* and in the PAPILIONIDAE section he marveled at the huge deep orange *Papiio antimachus.*

Yet on each wall, the spy noticed, there was an empty spot. A label was attached—he could read *Charaxes acraeoides.* But there was no such mounted butterfly.

Stealthily, in his little notebook, he wrote the name of the missing butterfly.

"I notice that one of your specimens is out for cleaning, sir," he commented.

The king looked up from Volume B of the encyclopedia. He saw that the spy was referring to the empty places on the shelves. His face fell.

"Missing. Rare," the king explained. "Hard to acquire. Working on it."

And so the spy went back to Duke Desmond's principality with the knowledge of how money could, indeed, buy happiness, at least when happiness took the form of a rare butterfly. His fellow spy was glum, having acquired nothing but an order for three hundred bottles of shampoo and three hundred bottles of curling lotion. "Funnels," he muttered. "I'll have to do it with funnels."

"Do what?" They were riding their horses side by side behind the cart that carried their samples.

"Fill six hundred bottles with soapy water."

"You could just forget it. Often people order things that never arrive."

The hair product spy considered that. Then he sighed. "Have you ever visited the dungeon?"

"Oh. Yes. I see what you mean."

"Filled with people who did not fulfill promises."

"Yes."

"Dark and cold and lonely."

"Yes."

"I'll use funnels. And you?"

"I got lucky. I'll tell the duke he has to send someone to find and buy that butterfly"—he took out his notepad and read the name of the missing specimen—"whatever the cost."

Back in his bedchamber, Duke Desmond was examining his clothing and deciding what to wear to the Birthday Ball. Green was good on him, he thought. Seductive. Maybe Spandex, which would outline his rounded stomach in an attractive way. Tights, probably. And pointed shoes. Yes, definitely: pointed shoes.

8.
The Schoolhouse

Her second day of school was less strange than the first, because the princess was part of the class now—she was the pupil Pat—and the other students accepted her as one of them.

They were all ages. She was probably the oldest, though two of the boys were as tall and had deepening voices. Most of the girls were middle-size, the age at which girls played with dolls and jump ropes (she had watched them at recess, and had held the frayed rope at one end when they asked her to help turn it), and one girl, Liz, the tiniest in the school, was no more than five, with large blue eyes, an infectious giggle, and a runny nose.

Liz's desk was next to Pat's. The little girl held her tongue between her lips in concentration, and she was practicing making letters on her paper. Her bare feet dangled, her legs too short to reach the floor, and she frequently pulled her skirt up to scratch a mosquito bite on her leg.

"You should put some lotion on that bite," Pat whispered to her.

The child wrinkled her nose and thought about it. "Dunno what lotion is," she said. "Never heared of such a thing."

In the castle an entire room was devoted to remedies, every-thing from headache potions to snakebite salves. A gray-haired apothecary was always there to dispense what one might need, and he could also apply leeches and pull teeth if nec-essary.

But of course, the prin-cess realized, a poor peas-ant had no room of remedies, no apothecary, no lotions.

"Oh, dear," she replied to the little girl. "I happen to have some, though I am a very humble and needy peasant myself. Tell your ma I'll bring something for you tomorrow, and you won't have to scratch so frequently."

Liz looked up from her misshapen As and Bs. "Got no ma," she said matter-of-factly.

"Oh, my! Pity! Well, your pa, then. Tell him."

"Got no pa neither."

"But—"

"I be a norphan," Liz explained.

An orphan! The princess knew of such people— she had heard stories about them. They frequently appeared in fairy tales. But here was one in person!

"But where do you live? Who takes care of you?" The princess couldn't imagine being so small and having no one.

"Oh," the little girl explained matter-of-factly, "I stay wif whoever wants me, 'cause they fink mebbe I can help out. Then, when they don't want me no more, I go live wif sumbody else."

"You must be very forsaken and pathetic," the princess said sympathetically. "I'm actually quite interested in orphans, and—"

She felt a sharp tap upon her shoulder and realized that a shadow had fallen across her desk.
The schoolmaster was standing beside her and had
used his pointing stick to tap her into attention.

"Sorry, sir," she said quickly, and looked down
at the geography book she was supposed to be
studying. An outline map showed all the domains,
and beyond them the seas, which were dotted with
small, intricately rendered drawings of serpents
and whales rising from the foam.

The other children laughed at her lunch. On her
first day, the day before, she had brought none, and
they had nicely shared torn-off bits of their own
thick bread. One, the pudgy boy named Fred, had
given her his apple. She had never eaten a whole
one before, because at the castle apples were always served peeled and sliced and arranged on a
porcelain plate.

"How primitive this is!" the princess said in delight as she bit through the skin, following the example of the others. "How peasant-y!"

"What?" Fred asked.

"I just meant blimey, what a good-tasting apple!" the princess explained, and dabbed some juice from her chin.

"Aye. I'll bring you another tomorrow. I got a whole apple tree by my house."

And he had. She thanked him for it and added it to the lunch she had brought today, her own castle breakfast wrapped in a napkin.

"What you got there?" one girl, Nell, asked, staring at her lunch.

"It's toast. Just bread, same as you, but toasted over a fire."

"And cut in fancy pieces!" Nell pointed out, laughing. She called the other girls to see—"Looky what Pat's got here in her lunch!"—and they all giggled. The princess, looking at her own cold toast, realized that peasant bread would not be cut into neat triangles as this was. She had so much to learn about being humble and poor.

"I just did it to be silly and foolish," she explained, and laughed with them, at the same time hiding the crisp bacon under her napkin.

"Where be your lard?" Nell asked.

"Lard?"

"Your pig fat, to rub on the bread. Blimey, I got lots! Want some of mine?"

The princess looked with horror at the glistening thick glob of white fat that Nell graciously offered.

"Thank you," she said, "but, ah, my belly's full. Just room for apple." She folded her napkin around the toast and bacon, bit into the bright red apple skin, and was relieved to see the lard disappear back into Nell's lunch.

"Pat!" The tiny waif, Liz, came scampering to her from the bushes that ringed the schoolyard. "I had me a bird," she wailed, "what I was taming with scraps of me lunch bread, to be a pet, so I would have sumfing to cuddle! Now I fink a cat has gone and et him!"

"Oh, no!" the princess cried. "Did you see it happen?" She looked to where the child was pointing and saw her own pet lying spread out, bulging belly exposed, in the sun.

"No. But the cat's got fevvers stuck to his whiskers. Blue ones, like me bird."

The princess sighed. "It's Delicious."

Liz burst into tears. "Mebbe it is to a cat, but it was me pet bird he et!"

The princess patted her back, attempting to comfort her, planning at the same time how to provide the orphan with . . . what was it she had said she wanted? Something to cuddle.

One of the advantages of being royalty was that, though life was boring, it did provide an opportunity to acquire anything one wanted. She could easily get a pet for this lonely child. She could order a singing bird, even a pair of them, perhaps in a gilded cage. But how to get them to little Liz anonymously?

She needed to give it some more thought. But now the bell was ringing. She could see the schoolmaster (and he *was* handsome, she thought, very handsome indeed, even if Tess the chambermaid *had* said he had a fierce face!) standing on the

steps, shaking the bell to summon them back to their desks.

He detained her at the end of the school day. "Pat?" he said. "I'd like you to stay for a minute, if you will."

The other pupils filed nervously past her on the

way to the door. "Punishment," one whispered sympathetically. "Hope it don't be too harsh."

Punishment? The princess had never been punished for anything, never in her life.

Apprehensively she waited at her desk until the schoolroom was empty. The schoolmaster, who stood at the door at the end of each day to say goodbye to his students, strode past her to his tall desk at the front. She noticed, again, his soft leather shoes, and remembered what Tess the chambermaid had confided, that the schoolmaster was part of a noble family in another kingdom, though he pretended otherwise.

His mouth was set in a firm line and his brow was furrowed so that he looked very stern when he summoned her to his desk.

"Come forward," he said curtly.

Odd, the princess thought, how often *she* had been the one to summon and command. How easy it was to do that. How hard, how demeaning, to be the one summoned! One didn't know exactly what to do, or where to look. She stood before him, her hands at her sides, and she looked at the floor and her own bare feet. Then, as an afterthought, she curtsied.

"Yes, sir," she said.

"I wanted to speak to you privately," he said, "about your schoolwork."

"Sir," she replied, "I'll try harder. I'm new, and didn't know the way to go about things, and so I skipped ahead in the book. I knew I shouldn't, but the pictures of sea serpents? I never been near no sea but I was interested in them things, and I skipped ahead without permission. I won't do it again, sir, no, I won't."

Then she curtsied once more.

He was staring at her.

She continued her lengthy apology. "And I know I kept leaning across to the orphan when she was working on her circles. I just thought I could help, sir! She's a pathetic orphan and has no ma nor pa what could help her at home. Also she has mosquito bites, sir, what itch her fiercely.

"I'm a poor peasant girl, remember, sir, and I hope you won't whip me, 'cuz my pa was killed by a something—a lion? No, a wild boar, it was.

"I'll try harder," she said again, and then fell silent.

The schoolmaster pulled out his handkerchief and held it to his mouth. His shoulders shook for a moment. Then he folded his handkerchief and looked sternly at her, his mouth set again in a line.

"I simply wanted to commend you, Pat," he said. "Your schoolwork is quite extraordinary. I don't know where you came from, or where you attended school before—"

"Some other domain. I forget what."

"Be that as it may, you were well taught. How old are you, Pat?"

"Soon sixteen, sir." *Four days,* she thought.

He frowned, thinking. "I was sixteen when I left the village school and went far distant to study at a teachers' academy. You might think about preparing to do the same. I could help you with the preparation, if you like."

"But I'm a girl, sir," the princess pointed out. "A poor peasant one," she added. "Very humble and pathetic."

"Yes, well, I understand that. But there were *some* girls at the teachers' academy. So although unusual, it is not unheard of.

"You might like to think about it. That's all. You may go now, Pat."

"Yes, sir, I will do that, I'll think about it, when I have time, though right now I must hurry back to

my hut, I mean my hovel, to help with the . . ."
Desperately the princess tried to remember what
hard-working peasants actually did. "Pigs. That's
it. I must tend the pigs, a very dirty and thankless
job, and I believe I might milk a cow as well, sir,
quite hard on the hands, and what's the other? Yes!
Collect firewood. I must bend over and get a very
achy back, collecting firewood; oh, it's a difficult
life, indeed, sir."

She looked up at last and saw that he was laughing.

"Blimey," she said, without thinking, "you're
wicked handsome when you laugh, sir!"

Then she curtsied and fled.

9.

The Prince

*P*rince Percival of Pustula dressed entirely in black, always. Even his underclothing was black. His hair had once been a nondescript brown, but he kept it dyed jet black and thickly oiled. His mustache, as well.

Black matched the darkness of his moods—he was always depressed—and, in fact, the color matched his heart. Percival was a black-hearted man who hated his subjects, the Pustulans, the populace of his domain; who hated his own family (he had sentenced his own mother to a minimum-security prison seven years before and he did not venture there on visiting days, never had, not once, and on the most recent Father's Day he had given his aged father a tarantula); and who, in truth, hated everyone but himself.

He spent a great deal of time in front of the mirror. He had had his own bedchamber lined with mirrors so that he could view himself from every angle. He preened. He strutted.

"Right hip? Ah, *yes*," he cooed to his own image on a sunny morning as he stood sideways in his underwear and observed his own stance and the jut of his hipbone.

"Pecs?" he murmured, and changed his position so that he could see the muscles of his chest bulge around the shoulder straps of his black silk undershirt. "Oh, *niiicce*," he said admiringly, turning slightly to the left and then to the right.

He smoothed his hair and then wiped his hand free of the hair oil, using the bedsheet and leaving a smear of black dye. He looked at his clothing, draped over a nearby chair. As he did so, he bellowed, "Valet!"

A valet is a sort of manservant, the one who tends the wardrobe and the needs of a nobleman. The Prince of Pustula's valet was a thin, mild-mannered middle-aged man who had, astonishingly, no name. Once, he had. His parents, upon his birth, had named him Hal. He had been Hal through his school years and during his quite successful career as an importer of Far East goods.

Then, unfortunately, he had been summoned before the prince because of a tiny snag in a pair of black silk socks imported from Asia. Hal the importer had been terrified by the summons. He knew what such a command had meant to others in the past. There were egg suppliers in exile, dentists in dungeons, and even a trouser presser locked away in a tower, all because of small flaws in their work.

Trembling, he had gone before the prince and knelt, as was required. Prince Percival flung the snagged sock at him and shouted obscenities.

Feeling he had nothing to lose, Hal picked up the sock and examined it while the prince continued to roar and shriek. With his thumb and fore-finger, he repaired the tiny snag by pushing a thread through and then smoothing it straight. Then, with his head bowed, he held the flawless sock up in a conciliatory and supplicating gesture.

The prince grabbed it. He looked at it. He turned it over and over in his thin-fingered hands.

"It's fixed!" he shouted.

"Yes, sir."

"It was unfixable!"

Hal did not know what to say. It was against the law not to answer the prince. But it was also against the law to answer him with a no.

In desperation he replied, "Yes, sir," agreeing (though he knew it was not true) that the sock had been unfixable.

"You performed a haberdashery miracle!"

Hal did not know what the word *haberdashery* meant. He *did* know he had not performed a mir-acle. But at this point he felt he had no choices left. *Lie or be executed,* he thought.

"Yes, sir," he said.

"You will be my new valet! Your new name is Valet!"

And thus Hal's future had changed. Once he had been a successful, well-traveled man, with business contacts in many domains. He had owned a camel and a horse. He had several maids. He had hoped to become affianced soon, to the daughter of a rug merchant.

But now he was a lowly valet and even his name had disappeared.

On this morning, summoned by the prince's bellow, he hurried into the room carrying his valeting equipment.

"Dress me," the prince commanded.

The valet bowed and began. First he opened the small suede bag that he carried and removed a soft brush with lemur-hair bristles. He picked up the black satin shirt with voluminous sleeves that was draped over the corner of the chair, examined it, brushed it meticulously, then held it while the prince slid his arms into the sleeves, shivering with delight at the feel of the sleek fabric. The valet buttoned the shirt and its cuffs as the prince gazed at himself in the mirror.

Next the valet lifted the velvet trousers from the chair and brushed them assiduously. He took out a perfumed spray from his bag and sprayed the trousers. He examined each button and tested the zipper.

Then, convinced, to his relief (for he worried terribly each morning), that the trousers were in perfect condition, he knelt and held them discreetly in just the right position for the prince to insert his legs, one after the other.

He raised the trousers and slipped the suspenders over the satin-covered shoulders of the prince.

Prince Percival posed in front of the mirror, flexing one knee at a time, to assess the fit.

"Mmm, *marvelous* thighs," the prince murmured to his own image. He tossed his head, looked into the mirror again, and shouted, "Brush, idiot!"

The valet hurried forward with his second brush, a smaller one made from the hair of a tapir's tail. Gently he brushed the prince's shoulders, which in the few short moments since he had been clothed had become peppered with white flakes of dandruff. It was an affliction of the prince's for which there seemed no remedy, and despite the thick lubricants with which he coated his dyed hair, the dandruff still fell like a perpetual blizzard.

Part of the valet's job was to accompany the

prince everywhere, brushing his shoulders unob-
trusively at intervals.

The prince leaned forward toward the mirror,
fingering his mustache and examining his pores.
"I'm planning to marry," he told his valet.

The valet tried to hide his surprise. Who would
marry the prince? He couldn't imagine. "I'm
pleased to hear that, sir," he said, and leaned forward to brush away a fresh torrent of flakes. "Will
you be making a public announcement?"

"I have to press my suit first," the prince replied. He leaned even closer to the mirror. "Toothpick!" he bellowed suddenly. The valet handed him
an ivory toothpick and waited while the prince
probed his teeth, found a morsel left from breakfast, examined it, and then ate it a second time.
The valet took the used toothpick and wrapped it
in a cloth, to be sterilized. He brushed the prince's
left shoulder.

"Just tell me which suit, sir. I have the ironing
board at the ready in the laundry room. I'll press
your suit."

Prince Percival whirled toward him, spraying
dandruff everywhere. "IMBECILE!" he shouted.

Terrified, the valet stepped back.

"I'm a *suitor!* Got that, you half-wit moron? SUITOR!"

"Yes, sir. I understand, sir." (He didn't, really.)

"Pressing my suit means that I must go through the formality of *wooing* my intended. It's a tedious, ridiculous bit of nonsense. But I will be going to a ball on Saturday night, to press my suit. Got it, idiot? To *press my suit!*"

"Yes, sir. I see, sir."

The valet stepped out of saliva range. Each time the prince said a word that began with the letter *p,* saliva accompanied the sound. Between the flying dandruff and the globs of spewing liquid—and in addition to the clouds of foul-smelling breath—the valet felt as if he were being attacked by airborne weaponry. He hoped the prince would not say anything else that began with the letter *p.*

The prince, calmer now, smoothed his oiled hair and practiced some slow smiles in the mirror: teeth exposed, teeth partially exposed, teeth concealed. He wasn't certain which smile to use on his intended when they met at the ball. They were all, he thought, so attractive.

"Wouldn't you like to know the name of my intended?" he asked the valet.

"Yes, sir, I would."

The prince sighed with pleasure, releasing a particularly terrible cloud of bad breath. "Princess Patricia Priscilla. We will be Prince Percival and Princess Patricia Priscilla, a perfect pair," he said.

The valet excused himself politely and rushed to the bath chamber to wash the saliva from his face.

10.
Dinner Conversation

Dinner in the castle was always a tedious meal, with many courses served one after another, and the king, queen, and princess seated so far from one another at the long mahogany table that it was difficult for them to converse. Not that it mattered. The queen's hearing was so poor that she misunderstood most of what was said, and the king was so preoccupied with thoughts of butterflies that he didn't care.

But on this evening, the second day after she had become a pupil-in-disguise at the village school, and four days before her Birthday Ball, the princess wanted to make a request of her parents.

"Father?" the princess said. But he didn't look up.

"Mother?" But the queen continued to sip at her soup and made no reply.

The princess gestured to the serving girl who stood near her chair. It was the alto, one of the three identical kitchen maids who sang together so beautifully in the kitchen.

"Yes, miss?" The serving girl curtsied.

The princess, hearing the deep timbre of the serving girl's voice, which she had never noticed before, remembered what Tess had told her about the music in the kitchen.

"Are you the one who sings?" the princess asked.

The serving girl blushed. "Yes, miss, but only in the kitchen. Never above-stairs, I promise."

"And those two? Are they the ones who sing with you? My chambermaid told me."

The other two sisters looked up. One stood at the far end of the table behind the king, and the other behind the queen at the opposite end. They noticed that the princess had pointed them out, and looked nervous.

"Yes, miss. More soup, miss? I can ring for the pulley boy to send some. Or there's pheasant pie next, quite lovely."

"No, no. I've had quite enough soup. I would like you to do something, though."

"Yes, miss."

"I would like to converse with my parents, but I can't seem to get their attention. Would you and the others—are they your sisters, by the way?"

"Yes, miss. Triplets, we are, all three of us born together in a whoosh whoosh whoosh, our ma said, such a surprise, but too many to feed. So now we're serving maids and take our meals for free."

"I was asking about singing. Is it true, what my chambermaid told me, that you sing?"

"Yes, miss, it is that."

"Well, would you and your sisters please sing something rousing? An attention-getting song?"

The serving girl looked stricken. "Oh, miss, it simply ain't allowed. Never never never. To sing above-stairs."

"Nonsense. I order it. Let me hear a first note."

Trembling, the girl hummed a note. *Hmmmmm.* Even though it was a small, frightened hum, the princess could hear the rich tone of her voice.

"Louder, please."

Hmmmmmm.

The two other serving girls looked over in

surprise, and then each one hummed in harmony. *Hmmmm. Hmmmm. Hmmmmm.* Their voices, together, blended into an exquisite sound. The king and queen, looking quite startled, both put down their soup spoons.

"It's all right! I've given them permission! I ordered them to do it!" the princess called to her parents in explanation.

"What?" the queen asked. "They've been given persimmons?"

"Permission," the king explained loudly. "Our daughter. Permission. Ordered them."

"I see," the queen replied, still confused.

"Once more," the princess said to the serving girls. "Move closer together."

Timidly the three girls moved to stand in a row. *Hmmmm. Hmmmm. Hmmmmm.* They hummed the three-part harmony once again.

"Do you do words?" the princess asked. "Or just hums?"

"Oh, all sorts of words, miss. *Tra-la*s and such, as well."

One of the sopranos giggled. "*Fiddle-de-fee*s, on occasion," she said.

"I'd like you to compose a song about the Birthday Ball. Maybe it could be a kind of, well, a celebration song."

"We could do a 'Happy Birthday to You,' miss. We do it all the time in the kitchen. It's always somebody's birthday. Cook's, last Thursday."

The princess frowned. "No. That's too ordinary. I'd like an original celebratory song."

"Yes, miss. We'll practice one down in the scullery. Shall I call for the pheasant pie now?"

"Oh, I suppose so. Sing for it, though."

The three serving girls grinned. They moved to the bell rope, which alerted the pulley boy, and one of the girls pulled on it. Then they opened the door in the wall and sang down to the kitchen:

"Pheasant pie! Pheasant pie! Pheasant pie!"

From below, echoing up through the passageway carved through three floors of thick stone, a baritone replied in song: *"Pheasant piiiiieee!"* and with the pulley boy's voice they could hear a small staccato accompaniment, the elderly serving boy tapping in time on the stone wall with a heavy fork. The rope moved, and dinner ascended.

Still singing *"Pheasant pie,"* the three girls served it, a plateful apiece, with some asparagus, and spooned some hollandaise on top.

"Sauce! Sauce! Sauce!" they sang in chorus.

"Now that I have your attention, Mother and Father, I would like to talk about the Birthday Ball," the princess said as the plates were served.

"Move closer so that I can hear you," the queen suggested. Then she turned to her husband. "You too, dear. Let's sit side by side and discuss the Birthday Ball.

"Girls?" she said, turning to the three serving maids, who curtsied, one by one, in reply. "Move our plates and forks and everything here together. Then, if you would, please hum lightly while we finish our dinner. It soothes my nerves and makes the meal seem festive."

"The entire village?" the queen asked, disconcerted. "To your Birthday Ball? Did I hear you correctly?"

"Yes, please, Mother. I'd like that." Princess Patricia Priscilla touched the tip of her silver fork to the pale yellow sauce. "The villagers are all poor peasants and they have never been to a ball. Think how they'd enjoy it."

"Oh, I don't know, I don't know," the queen murmured. "It's so not done."

"Father? What do you think?"

The king had begun to tire of talk about the ball and his mind had wandered off to contemplate rare butterflies. He frowned. "What do I think. About what. I don't know. No idea. Not a clue."

"Might I invite the villagers to my Birthday Ball?" the princess asked him patiently.

"Villagers. Ball. Whatever." The king's mind was on the rare butterfly that was missing from his collection. Perhaps if he arranged a jungle excursion . . .

"We would have to order them to wash first," the queen mused.

"Peasants are clean, Mother—truly, they are." The princess took a small bite of asparagus. "But of course we could mention bathing, in the invitation, if you think we should."

"Mention what? What was that? Baiting? Oh, I don't think so, dear. There was a terrible sport in the old days, called bearbaiting. Your father outlawed it years ago."

"*Bathing,* Mother. We could say that the invitation is for all well-bathed villagers." The princess enunciated clearly.

"Yes, of course. Bathing." The queen nodded. "I'd hope they wouldn't bring gifts, though, dear. Think what they might bring. Piglets, I'm afraid . . . things like that."

"We would tell them gifts aren't necessary, Mother. In fact . . ."

"The suitors will bring gifts, of course. Oh my, I make myself nervous and excited, just thinking what incredible gifts the suitors might bring!" The queen shivered.

The princess did not want to think about, or talk about, suitors. "In fact," she went on, "I would like to give gifts to the villagers."

"Eh? What was that? Gift gifts? Give gives? Give gloves? Lift cloves? Oh, dear, I can't think what ever you are talking about."

"Father?" The princess turned to the king. "May I have your permission to give gifts to the villagers?"

"Gifts. Permission. Yes. Whatever. I'll skip dessert." The king took his linen monogrammed napkin from his lap and gestured to the serving girls, who hurried to the table to remove his plate.

The queen wiped her lips daintily with her own napkin and then nodded to one of the triplets. "Do hum a bit more," she said. "Or sing. I did enjoy that."

Holding a tray with the waiting dessert dishes on it, the alto sang, *"Apricot ice cream . . ."* and the other girls joined in:

"Apricot ice cream . . ."

"Apricot ice cream . . ."

The king changed his mind. "Changed my mind. Dessert. After all."

The three serving girls continued singing as they served the ice cream and then left the dining chamber, carrying trays of empty plates, and descended the stairs. Their harmony grew fainter as they walked to the kitchen.

From far below, in the antechamber to the kitchen, the sound echoing through the pulley passage, the princess heard the pulley boy join in with his deep, rich baritone. *I do hope Tess is down there, hearing that,* the princess thought, thinking of the freckled chambermaid.

Then she heard a sweet female voice join in and knew that Tess was right there in the middle of the music.

11.

The Conjoint Counts

When the conjoint counts were born and were revealed to be joined at the middle, which was quite astonishing to their parents, a royal decree was issued almost immediately. It seemed fairly simple, not designed to cause hardship.

Everything in the domain was to become plural in name. The word *cow*, a word commonly used in the area because there were many farms, was now to be *cows*.

It was sometimes difficult for the peasants. They were accustomed to saying "Do your lessons," or "Pull up your trousers," but they had a hard time remembering to say, "Go milk the cows" when the family owned only one. Now, instead of weeding the garden, they had to weed the gardens, even though they were tending only a small patch of carrots and potatoes. And when a peasant mother told her little ones, "Go and kiss your granny," she was required to say, "Go and kiss your grannies," which confused the tots and made them cry, often, and refuse their supper.

Even now, though years had passed since the decree, and though the parents of the conjoint counts were long dead, the language of the domain continued to make use of the superfluous plural. No one was ever quite certain what verb to employ. In speaking of a single tree, for example, should one say "The trees is large" or "The trees are large"? Small children had trouble learning to talk. It was a nuisance and a bother—sometimes worse—but it was the Law of the Domain.

Count Colin and Count Cuthbert were adults now, and ruled the domain in which they lived. But although they were joined at the middle, always had been, always would be, it did not make them the best of friends. They agreed on only one thing, and that was jokes. They both laughed uproariously at bathroom jokes, or jokes involving underwear, though as soon as they finished laughing, they argued about who could tell a joke better, and sometimes made rude noises at each other with their lips, and said "Nyah nyah" and "I'm rubber, you're glue, everything you say bounces off me and sticks to you" in a singsong, whiny voice.

They had a particular annoying prank that they played on each other. One would wait until his brother's face was turned toward his own, and then belch loudly at it and cry, "Gotcha!"

The belched-at one would invariably respond with a full-scale wedgie.

They bickered constantly. If Colin wanted to walk to the left, Cuthbert insisted that *right* was the way to go, so that they pulled at each other and argued.

Their clothing was, of course, specially made, with four arms and four legs and two neckholes and a very wide waist—called, of course, a waists—to accommodate them both. But if Colin decided to wear the blue suit, Cuthbert said no, the brown. Then they fought, and had even torn some suits to shreds. Once they had decided to be naked for an entire day because they couldn't agree on what to wear.

If Cuthbert wanted to sleep, Colin decided not only to stay awake but to play his saxophones (of course he played only one, but he spoke of it, as required, in the plural) fortissimo so that the blares kept his brother awake and angry.

Colin was squeamish about bugs, so Cuthbert collected them, and kept the pockets on his side of their specially made trousers filled with crickets and beetles and things that squirmed and occasionally made noises.

Cuthbert had grown what he called a beards. Of course it was only one beard, and he thought it quite handsome. Colin was not only clean-shaven but very ticklish, and his brother's beard constantly brushed against his neck with its wiry, curling ends, making him shriek.

When they attended church, as rulers generally do, they were a distraction for the populace. When

Colin wanted to kneel, Cuthbert wanted to stand. If Cuthbert decided to sing a hymn (or hymns, as it was called), it was at the very moment that Colin felt compelled to pray. With their constant pulling and tugging and shrieking and bickering, their poking and slapping and name-calling, the most solemn ceremonies were chaotic, and even an entire order of contemplative nuns had complained that they lost their ability to concentrate if the conjoint counts were in the congregation.

But like the Duke of Dyspepsia and the Prince of Pustula, the Counts of Coagulatia were immensely wealthy and overwhelmingly powerful. No one could change their behavior, or complain about it.

It was at an evensong service that those who had gathered in the cathedral noticed a change. The counts, sitting together as they always did, since there was no other way for them to sit, were relatively peaceful throughout the service. They knelt together, sang together, and even, the villagers noticed (because it was not the usual thing, or proper thing, in church), giggled loudly from time to time as if they had a secret.

"Something has happened to the conjoint counts," people murmured. "Wonder what!"

The murmurs reached the castle.

"What has happened to the conjoint counts?" was asked again and again, first of the guards at the portcullis, then by a food deliveryman with a crate of aubergines at the kitchen door, and once by a small child who wandered through the courtyard with his fingers in his mouth (or mouths, as he had been taught to say) so that the question came out slurpy and moist.

What has happened to the conjoint counts?

Finally the people were told. A royal proclamation was issued, with trumpets tootling and flower petals flung everywhere along the village lanes.

"The conjoint counts have chosen a brides!" was the announcement.

The villagers wondered exactly what that meant, and who the brides might be that would be willing to marry the pair of them, but no one dared to ask.

"I love her initials," Colin said with a wicked little laugh as they began to plan their journey to the neighboring domain where the Birthday Ball was being held for the princess. They were making a lists of things to take. "Pee pee."

"Pee pee poo poo," Cuthbert chortled. "I'm going to get new underwears and have it monogrammed like that." He began to write it on the list: **PP.**

"No, you can't! I thought of it first." Colin slapped his brother's hand so that the pencil fell to the floor.

Cuthbert pushed him. In no time they were back at it, shoving and poking as they always had, forgetting the brief friendship that their decision to marry the princess had forged.

"I'm going to burp on you!" Cuthbert said. "Big burps on the way!" He opened his mouth and belched at Colin, who, being attached, could not avoid it, though he turned his head away. "Gotcha! Smelled like our lunches, huh? Huh?"

"I'm going to tell her what a poopy-pants you are!" Colin said. "Then she won't want to—"

But they both fell silent. If the princess didn't want to marry one of them, she couldn't marry the other.

Sullenly they stopped jostling each other, picked up the pencil, went back to the list, and continued planning the journey and deciding what provisions they would need.

Colin looked at what had been written already, gave a hoarse chuckle, and poked Cuthbert in the ribs with his elbow. "Know what? Know where we're going? Huh? Huh?"

Cuthbert poked him back. "Huh?"

"Balls!" Colin said.

"Balls!" Cuthbert echoed with a rude gleeful laugh.

For a moment they were quite peaceful together, thinking how amusing it would be to announce their presence by bellowing "Balls!" when they arrived, and then to explain their intentions to become Patricia Priscilla's husbands.

12.

The Invitation

The invitation from the castle, elaborately decorated, arrived in the village on Thursday. It was delivered to each cottage and each farmhouse and, finally, to the schoolhouse.

The princess noticed with relief that the message boy, an old man who had been doing the same job for the castle for many, many years—he had been the one, almost sixteen years before, to deliver the announcements of the birth of the princess, and five years before that, the marriage of the king and queen—did not recognize her in her peasant garb. He was old, and his eyesight was poor. He simply squinted into the schoolhouse, glanced around at the pupils all working at their desks, and then hobbled forward with his cane to deliver the rolled scroll to the schoolmaster.

"From the castle," he said abruptly. There was no reason to add the word "sir" to a lowly village schoolmaster. And, too, he was tired. He had delivered so many announcements over so many years, and now suffered from boredom, arthritis, and a trick knee. He also needed spectacles.

"Thank you," the schoolmaster said, in some surprise, but when he looked up, the message boy had already turned and hobbled out. He had several more deliveries to make and was eager to finish.

"I wonder what this could be!"

The pupils all called out guesses. "Maybe a notice that you forgot to pay yer rent!" called Fred.

"No, part of my salary for being schoolmaster is the room where I live," the schoolmaster explained.

"Announcement of a traveling circus comin' around?" suggested Nell hopefully, for there had been one once, and she remembered all of it: the ringmaster in a bright red costume with gold buttons, a monkey wearing a hat, and a white dog that danced.

"Usually," the schoolmaster reminded them, fingering the rolled message, "a traveling circus is announced by jesters who come cartwheeling through the village the day before, selling tickets."

"Maybe it's an order to witness a whipping!" was Mick's hope, for he was interested in violence, always, so long as he was not on the receiving end. There had not been a public whipping in a long time, not since the day a very bad-tempered village woman had smashed all of her neighbor's best pots in a fit of anger after an argument about who made the best stew. It hadn't been much of a whipping, either, just a few taps to remind her to hold her temper in check.

The little orphan, Liz, scratched her mosquito bite, smeared now with lotion that the princess had provided. She leaned forward and tried to peer at the mysterious paper. Then she closed her eyes tight and held her breath, the ritual for making a wish. "Oh, I do hope a circus," she whispered. "I never once seen one."

"It's an invitation," the princess said under her breath. She watched while the schoolmaster unrolled the message.

Birthday Banquet and Ball!
For the Princess Patricia Priscilla!

༄

Saturday Night at the Castle
Food • Gifts • Music • Suitors
Villagers Welcome!
(Please Bathe)

The schoolmaster held it up so that the children could see, and they called out the words.

"What's a suitor, sir?"

The schoolmaster explained the concept of suitors, and they all wrinkled their noses.

"What's gifts?" asked Liz.

So he explained gifts. None of the pupils had ever received a gift. Their eyes grew wide. "Blimey," said Nell. "They gives you sumpthin'? And you don't got to work for it?"

"I expect it will be just a *small* gift," the princess said. "I mean, because we're poor miserable peasants and all. Perhaps just a small candy, or a toy?"

"A candy? A *toy?*" the children shouted.

"What's a toy?" asked little Liz.

"When's Saturday?" asked Ben, who could never remember such things.

"Day after tomorrow!" everyone cried out in delight. "Day after tomorrow!"

The princess lingered after school was dismissed for the day. She had begun to dread returning to the lonely castle, and so she volunteered to sweep the floor and arrange the books and papers in order. Tidying things, she glanced surreptitiously at the schoolmaster, who sat at his desk, correcting the spelling tests they had done that morning.

He looked up at her. "Will you be attending the Birthday Ball, Pat?" he asked.

She sighed. She knew that Saturday would mean the end of her schoolhouse life, the end of her days posing as a peasant.

"Yes, sir," she said. "And you, sir?" she asked. "Will you be going, and getting a gift? Blimey, I suppose you never got no gift before, sir." She made the observation slyly, knowing that the schoolmaster was really not a common peasant at all, because the chambermaid had told her of the high origins of Herr Gutmann. She wondered if he would confess to her now who he was.

But he did not. "No," he replied. "There have been no gifts in my life."

She teased him a bit. "Aw, sir, surely your ma gave you sumpthin'? A play horsie carved of wood?"

His look was sad. "My ma died when I was just a small boy," he told her.

"Oh, sir! A pity, that! Was she killed like my ma, by a—what was it, then? A wild dog?"

"You once said a boar, Pat, and that it was your pa who died."

"Oh! I did indeed, and it was that, a boar killed my pa. I forgot for a minute. A boar killed my pa, and my ma does laundry, and that's the truth."

"My mother died after giving birth to my sister," the schoolmaster said, "and my little sister is gone as well—my pa sent her away—so I have lost them both."

"Blimey, that was cruel of yer pa!"

"I no longer think of him as Pa. He disowned me when I went off to become a teacher. Too uppity, he said. Putting on airs, he called it."

"But, sir!" She caught herself. She had almost revealed that she knew of his noble origins. Something stopped her. He looked too sad.

"I'm finished here, sir. I'll be off now."

He nodded, looking down again at the spelling papers. She hoped that her careful misspellings looked real and that he—for one more day, until the ball, which she so dreaded—would continue to think her an uneducated girl, a humble peasant in need of his teaching.

Outside the schoolhouse, the princess called to her waiting pet. She had been feeding Delicious extra sardines so that the cat would not sadden the orphan by eating birds. Now she could see, as Delicious woke up and rolled over, in response to her call, that the additional rations were having an effect. The cat was developing quite a tummy.

"Your size is ambitious, Delicious," she said, but her mind was really elsewhere and the fun of her own wordplay was diminished. She walked slowly back to the castle, the cat at her heels, thinking about how the village world would be lost to her after the ball. Briefly, too, she thought with despair about the impending arrival of the suitors.

13.
The Kitchen

The huge kitchen and its anterooms were alive with bustle and noise. There was no music now, except for the quiet sounds from a pantry corner where the three serving girls, exempted from their regular duties, were working on the song they'd been commanded to prepare for the ball. Today it was the clank of kettles and the clatter of plates, the thunk of knives, the roar of the cooking fires, and the hurried footsteps of the many servants, all of it orchestrated by the barked commands of the cook.

"You! Pulley Boy!" she shouted.

"Yes, Cook?" The boy looked in from the hall-way where he always positioned himself near the pulley door. He was a tall boy with curly hair and bright blue eyes.

"Take a helper and go bring in the pigeons! There's two hundred of them waiting out by the back entrance, all of them with their necks fresh wrung."

"*Necks wrung,* Cook?" The pulley boy gulped. He liked birds, had even kept a few as pets back in the village, before he took this job.

"We can't eat 'em with their wings flappin', now can we?" she replied with a wide grin.

"Well, no, I guess not," the pulley boy acknowledged, though to himself he was wondering why anyone had to eat them at all. If he had his way, he would eat nothing but carrots and beans and bread. Maybe a fish now and then. He didn't like the thought of poor creatures becoming food. If any living thing had to have its neck wrung, he wished it were the princess's large yellow cat, which tended to hide behind draperies, then leap out and scratch the servants. Luckily the pulley boy rarely had call to go above-stairs. But he knew chambermaids with long scratches on their ankles from the claws of the cat.

"Delicious, you are so capricious," the princess

had been heard to say fondly, picking up the cat after it had attacked a footman one day.

"Blimey, that critter's savage," one pudgy girl had complained, returning to the kitchen with blood on her stockings.

Too bad we can't roast and eat cats, the pulley boy thought as he looked around for someone to help him bring in the birds. All of the regular kitchen staff was hard at work, chopping and simmering and parboiling and plucking. Some were counting pink salmon that were contained in a huge tub of water. One young chopping lad, an apprentice still, was doing nothing but truffles, mincing them into a large pile. Another had been assigned to peel asparagus and stood behind a mountain of green spears hardly knowing where to begin. Others were polishing silverware from enormous deposits on a long table.

The pulley boy was about to call on his little brother, who was playing with a marble near the bell wall, when a tall, freckled girl wearing a shabby dress under her apron volunteered shyly.

"I could go with you," the girl said.

"Get them goats on the spit!" Cook bellowed to the staff. "They have to cook all day and through the night!" She turned back to the kitchen, and the elderly serving boy, who usually tended only pets, shuffled reluctantly over to help lift the large goats that would be roasted for the banquet.

The pulley boy looked at the freckled, eager girl. He recognized her as the seventeenth chambermaid, the one who tended the princess and who sometimes, in the kitchen, joined in the singing with a sweet, clear voice. Then he looked at his brother, who continued to roll his green marble back and forth on the floor. "I suppose he should stay in case a bell is pulled," he mused, "though that girl—the princess?—she's off for the day somewheres. She hasn't called for lunch all week. And I already sent the queen's lunch aloft, and the king is in his counting house, so I don't think—"

"Your brother had better stay," the chambermaid said, "in case the butler pulls a bell cord or sumpthin'."

"Right, then. Come along." He gestured, and the girl followed him through the hall, chattering happily as they went. "Creamed pigeons, she's making," she told him. "Can you believe it? For two hundred! And some of them villagers, not nobility! I lived in the village once, and I never heard of a creamed pigeon—"

"I remember you did." He pushed open the heavy door.

"Remember I did what? Heard of a creamed pigeon? I never!"

"No. I remember you lived in the village. With your pa. I remember he beat you. Everyone knew."

The chambermaid grew flustered. "Well, he said I was a useless great galoomph, and I suppose I was."

"But you went to school. I used to see you going to the schoolhouse and your pa yelling after you, and throwing things sometimes."

The chambermaid nodded. "I did. I wanted to learn to read, and the schoolmaster taught me. He was very strict and rapped your knuckles if you didn't pay attention, but he taught me my letters and how to read! And now I'm reading the best book, about a girl named Alice, who has adventures you wouldn't believe! Maybe you could borrow it when I'm done!"

"Look: here they are. We should load them in the barrow, I suppose." They had stopped at the large pile of dead pigeons. The boy picked one up and looked at its staring eyes. After a moment he dropped it into the wooden wheelbarrow standing nearby. Then he sighed and reached for more. "I can't read. Worked all my life since I was a tot. Never went to school," he said. "Here: grab some. You said you'd help. Don't just stand there."

"Poor pidgies—they look like sumpthin' you'd feed the cat. Maybe with cream sauce, though . . ." The chambermaid leaned over, filled her apron with limp birds, and walked to the wheelbarrow. "My name's Tess," she told him, spilling the birds into it. "I could teach you, Pulley Boy."

"Cream sauce? No thanks."

"To read."

"You could do that?" He scooped up another armful of birds. Then he nodded to her, and blushed. "I'm John," he said.

"Pastry!" They could hear the cook shout in the kitchen. "Clear some tables for rolling out the pastry!"

"I could!" the chambermaid said. "It's easy. Look: *A* is first, all stiff and upright, like this." She drew the letter with a stick in the ground beside the wheelbarrow. The pulley boy, his arms filled with pigeons, stared down at it.

"*A* is for Alice, in that book I told you about."

He dropped the pigeons onto the top of the pile they had already made. "Lemme try it, then," he said, and took the stick from her. Carefully he made an *A* in the dirt.

"Nuts to be shelled!" the cook called. "Where's that boy went to get the pigeons? He could be shelling these pistachios!'"

Quickly they loaded the last of the limp birds and pushed the wheelbarrow toward the corridor. "I'll show you *B* later," Tess whispered.

"*B* is for *birthday,* and for *ball,*" she explained.

14.

The Suitors

From three different directions they started out, early Saturday morning, as the sun was rising. Each suitor had an entourage of servants, horses, a coach in which to ride, and long lines of bearers carrying trunks of clothing, toiletries, and trinkets.

A hawk, soaring high on the cloudless morning, peering below, his keen eyes alert for rodents or snakes to descend on for his breakfast, saw the processions from a great distance. From his place in the sky they looked like scores of ants moving steadily toward a destination where they would all converge on some edible mound, perhaps the leavings of a peasant picnic. But the hawk, no stranger to humans and the complicated lives they led, knew exactly what and who these caravans were.

Through the countryside they came. En route from the east, Duke Desmond of Dyspepsia lay back among the thick cushions in his carriage, snoring. In his sleep he scratched himself. His stomach grumbled noisily. From the side of his always open mouth, a bit of drool slid to the cushion and made a wet splotch.

Surrounding his carriage rode six attendants on horseback, each one selected for superior eyesight. They swiveled their necks constantly, searching the landscape for anything that might create a reflection. Their entire duties were to make absolutely certain that no mirror, no looking glass, nothing of a reflective nature, would ever be within range of Duke Desmond's vision.

When they approached a lake, the attendants signaled the procession to halt. Two of them rode ahead and perceived that the lake was quite still: not a dark stagnant pond, but rather a deep, serene pool of clear water.

They cantered to the shore, urging their horses until their noses were at the edge and, in fact, they leaned down to drink.

Seated on the horses' backs, the attendants leaned forward in their saddles, looked at their own reflections in the water, and sighed. It would never do.

"Splashers!" they called loudly back to the entourage. "Summon the splashers!"

Upon hearing the summons, a troop of thirty men wearing bathrobes trotted from the back of the procession, where they had been assigned to march, to the edge of the lake. This was their moment, the time they trained for. They got into position and in unison dropped their bathrobes, plunged naked into the water, and swam to their designated spots. Then with highly synchronized movements (they trained in a castle pool every morning) they splashed with their muscular arms, churning the water into a froth.

The procession started up and passed the lake slowly. Duke Desmond, pillowed in his carriage, had woken at the stopping and starting, and he heard the noise. He raised a window shade, glanced outside, and saw nothing but a body of water wild with waves, foam, and bubbles. It did not seem surprising to Desmond that on a clear sunny morning a lake would be so tempestuous. In his presence, all lakes were controlled by the splashers, and he had never seen one calm and reflective.

The duke closed the shade, yawned, gobbled several aspirin to soothe his toothache, scratched his left armpit, and tossed his thick dirt-encrusted hair from one side to the other. His manservant, poised, as he had been for hours, on a narrow, straight-backed seat, leaned forward to fluff the duke's pillows and murmured his usual greeting: "How fine you look this morning, sir!"

The lengthy procession moved along on the rutted road. As it passed the lake, the splashers quickly redonned their robes and trotted back into their marching place. The front attendants continued to scan the landscape vigilantly for anything that might be reflective. And at the very end, a uniformed man, especially chosen for his sure-footedness, marched very carefully, alert for any rock or hole that might cause him to stumble. He carried a bamboo cage that contained a very rare, very valuable butterfly. It would be the duke's gift, the gift that would amaze and delight the king, that would persuade the Princess Patricia Priscilla to choose him of all the suitors, and would make her the Duke of Dyspepsia's bride.

From the west, a similarly long and complicated procession moved forward from the domain of Pustula. There were the decorated horses, of course, the costumed courtiers, and the elaborate coach that carried Prince Percival and his valet. There was also a large brass band trained to form themselves, while marching and playing, into the shape of one large letter *P*, or, alternatively, into four *small* *P*s intended to represent the bride-and-groom-to-be.

In addition, trudging at the end of the line, a large number of servants were carrying trunks of the prince's clothing, boxes of ointments, jars of perfumes, and tubes of hair dyes and pomades, as well as whisk brooms to resupply the valet from time to time when his dandruff brushes became clogged and had to be destroyed.

Finally, surrounding the entire entourage, walking with precision, were one hundred mirror bearers. They walked sideways, like crabs—an art they practiced and practiced back in the domain when the prince was not traveling—so that at any given

moment, if the prince looked from the window of his carriage, he would not see scenery, not see lakes or hills or meadows, though they were traveling through such a landscape, but instead would behold with satisfaction the thing he most admired: himself.

Inside the carriage, at his side so that he could stroke it now and then (following which he curtly ordered the valet to wipe it free of his oily fingerprints), sat a small rectangular silver box with a lid that was snapped closed and latched. The box contained his engagement gift to the princess, the specially made gift that he knew would persuade her to agree to be his wife.

The procession of the conjoint counts was moving down from the north at the same time. But seen from the hawk's point of view, from above, it was a sharp contrast to the steady and orderly lines that came from the east and the west. The third group, equally large, moved in fits and starts, in zigs and zags.

It was because it had two leaders and they couldn't agree.

"Take that detours, there to the left!" Count Colin had bellowed, leaning from the left-hand window of the double-wide carriage in which he rode with his twin brother.

"No, stupid, go to the right!" Count Cuthbert shouted, and dragged his brother across the slippery leather seat of the carriage so that he could put his head through the window on the right, and point. In retaliation for being dragged, Colin yanked his brother's beard as hard as he could. Cuthbert turned and slapped him, then grabbed one of his brother's earlobes and twisted. The carriage lurched and jiggled as they fought, kicking and biting, and the entire procession once again, as it had throughout the day, slowed to a halt because the drivers did not know whether to go left or right.

"Sirs!" A polite knock at the carriage door interrupted the fight, and the convoy leader, an army general in full uniform, expressed his concern to the counts. "We're losing time because of all the stoppings and startings, and I fear we will arrive late for the balls if we don't move more steadily along."

"It's *his* fault!" Colin said, gesturing to his brother. "He caused all the poppings and fartings!"

He laughed raucously and poked Cuthbert with an elbow. "Get it? Get it?"

Cuthbert poked him back and giggled. "Poppings and fartings!" he repeated with glee.

The general waited patiently. "May I suggest, sirs, that in order to proceed at a good paces, we rely on the maps readers? I believe they have studied the routes carefully. We have entire troops of geography experts."

"Entire poops?" Colin chortled. "What do you think, Cuth? Shall we let the poops lead us, with their stoopy-poopy maps?"

Count Cuthbert put his tongue between his lips and made a rude noise at the general.

Count Colin turned, pulled down his trousers, and mooned the general.

Then they both leaned back in their seat and began to pick their noses. "Get moving!" Count Cuthbert called loudly to the carriage driver. "Me and Colin want to get married!"

The hawk, watching as the convoys advanced, sensed what was coming. They would converge, he could see, at the castle, and no good would come of it, no good at all.

He screeched and wheeled about in the cloudless sky, wanting nothing to do with humans, and especially these. He tested the wind, then turned and flew full-speed toward the southwest, deciding to soar today over a distant city instead, where he would find rats, a much more reliable species. You always knew exactly where you stood with a rat, and they were edible as well.

15.

Preparations

An entire room beside the banquet hall had been designated the gift room and was filled now with the wrapped and ribboned gifts that the princess would distribute to the villagers during dinner, before the toasts were made.

There were dolls and balls and kites and games for all the village children, and for those who attended school, a shiny sharpened pencil as well.

There were flowered aprons for the village housewives, each with a small bottle of perfume in the pocket. For the village men, most of them farmers, bright-colored handkerchiefs, and combs.

Special gifts had been chosen by the princess for special people. For Tess, her chambermaid, her own copy of *Alice in Wonderland,* with illustrations; for the schoolmaster, a leather-bound book of maps (in which she had inscribed, "For Herr Gutmann, with thanks from Patricia Priscilla, who was Pat for too short a time"); an engraved silver pitch pipe for the trio of singing serving girls, who would, tonight, perform the song that they had prepared for the birthday; for the pulley boy, a fine pair of gloves to protect his hands against the thick rope; and finally, for the little orphan who wanted something to cuddle, a small pink-ribboned basket containing a satin cushion with a note attached that read: "Coming soon: one delicious kitten."

(Upstairs, that morning, upon awakening, the princess had looked around, as usual, for her cat. A loud purr and some tiny squeaking sounds directed her attention to a far corner of the bedchamber, where she saw Delicious lying haughtily upon a pillow that had been dragged from a chair. The cat was licking and tending three tiny yellow kittens.

"I should have known!" the princess cried. "The size of your tummy was suspicious, Delicious!")

∾◦◦⌢

The sun was just beginning to set over the domain. Outside, on the castle grounds, scores of tents had been set up for the visitors who had traveled long distances. Beyond the vegetable gardens, spreading down toward the king's fishing creek, were the red striped tents that housed Duke Desmond and his many courtiers. It had been an unfortunate choice of location, for the splashers, already exhausted when they arrived, were immediately called into service once again. Now they took turns, going in groups of ten at a time, dashing to the creek to stir up the usually quiet waters.

On another side of the castle grounds, beside the meadow where wildflowers attracted hundreds of bees that lived in nearby hives and provided the honey for the queen's breakfast, green polka-dotted tents provided shelter for Prince Percival and his entourage. It too had been a poor choice, for the rows of tents, when surrounded by the mirror bearers, blocked the beeline to the meadow, which confused the bees dreadfully and was beginning to make them so angry that a sinister and alarming *bzzzzz* was becoming quite audible.

Finally, behind the counting house and west tower, a double-wide blue and white checked tent had been erected for the conjoint counts, and around it, similar but smaller blue and white tents for their many servers and carriers. But the large tent had already partially collapsed because of the wrestling match between Colin and Cuthbert that had ensued shortly after their arrival, when one wanted the bedpillows arranged to the east and the other to the west. Colin got Cuthbert in a hammerlock, but Cuthbert dug his fingernails into Colin's backside, and within moments they had destroyed the furniture and splintered one of the side tent poles.

"Oh, miss, you do look so lovely and grown up." Tess the chambermaid had just finished pinning up the princess's hair. Ordinarily it fell in curls over her shoulders. But tonight, for the first time, she would wear it on top of her head, framed by a small tiara of pearls and aquamarines that just matched her eyes.

"Well, Tess, I'm sixteen today." The princess sighed and leaned forward toward the looking glass to fasten earrings that matched the tiara. "Sixteen is grown up." She stared at herself and bit her lip. "Old enough to marry," she added in a small voice.

"Blimey," the chambermaid said. For a moment they were both silent.

"Oh, Tess!" The princess wiped away a small tear that had formed in the corner of her eye. "I did so love going to school! And the schoolmaster said he could help me to become a teacher!"

"Why don't you then, miss? That would be just the thing for you! I been thinkin' about wantin' to become a teacher myself, miss, someday! I tried teachin' the pulley boy his letters, and he took to it right away!"

"The Law of the Domain," the princess said sadly.

"Law of the Domain? What ever's that, miss?"

"It's—well, it's the law, Tess. It says the heiress—that's me—has to marry at sixteen and produce an heir, or another heiress."

"An air? Well, that's foolish, miss, to think you can produce an air. The *sky* does that. Or the heavens, maybe. Sumpthin' up there, anyways." The chambermaid went to the window and looked out. "Just see! The leaves are movin' around. There's plenty of air."

"No, an *heir,* Tess. It's not the same. It means a . . ."

The princess fell silent.

"A what, then?"

"A baby," the princess said in a small voice.

Tess looked outraged. "A baby! No way! Not now, miss! Not when you are sixteen and wantin' to be a teacher! Maybe later, miss! But not now!" The chambermaid paced angrily back and forth across the bedchamber.

The princess stood up, and her embroidered petticoats swirled around her. "Pull yourself together, Tess. It makes me fretful when you pace," she said with resignation. "It is the Law of the Domain, and it is my sixteenth birthday. Help me with my gown."

The chambermaid stamped her foot. "But blimey, miss, it's a bad law! Can't sumbody change it?"

"Only the king. My father."

Tess stood still. "A pa can be hard," she said. "Mine was. Threw me right out of the house, he did. Told me to not come back."

"My father's not cruel like that. He's a good ruler, I think. We haven't gone to war in years because he doesn't believe in it." The princess gestured to the silvery-blue gown that was laid out carefully on her bed.

"He never raises taxes," she went on, "and he outlawed hangings. Get the gown, Tess."

Tess carefully picked up the elaborate gown and lowered it over the princess, taking care not to muss the elegantly upswept hair. With her voice muffled by the heavy folds of the skirt, the princess continued, "He holds celebrations, and parades, and invites traveling circuses. Last year he built a *hhssspp*—"

"What's that, miss?" The chambermaid eased the gown down so that the head of the princess emerged.

"Hospital. He had a hospital built because he learned that the villagers had none. Do you remember when Cook chopped her hand, Tess, when she was aiming for a turkey? It was the hospital stitched her up so nicely."

"So they did, miss. Hardly a scar." The chambermaid began to button, one by one, the long line of pearl buttons on the back of the gown.

"He's a good king," the princess said again.

"Yes, he is, miss. Hold still."

"He loves me dearly."

"Don't squirm. I can't button when you squirm, miss."

"He only wants the best for me."

The chambermaid stopped buttoning and stood back indignantly with her hands on her hips. "Well then, miss," she said in a loud voice, "all I got to say is he has an odd way of showin' it iffen he wants you to have a air when you're still nothin' but a girl. I know he don't beat you like my pa did, or throw you out, but iffen he was a *really* good king he would change the Law of the Domain, and that's all I got to say, miss!"

A small golden clock on the dressing table chimed.

"Button, Tess. It's almost time."

"And as for them suitors, miss—well, we haven't talked about them suitors. But I *seen* them, miss, when they arrived. One is the ugliest man in the world, miss, with teeth that stick out and a huge snarl of dirty hair all ratted up. And the next one, miss, well, the next one don't do nuthin' but strut and look at hisself every minute, and his hair is sleeked back with foul-smelling oil. And the last one, miss, blimey, the last one is two stuck together, slapping at each other and spitting and using the coarsest language—"

"Tess, don't talk about them—I can't bear it!"

"But miss, they say you have to choose tonight! They say below-stairs that at the ball you have to choose, and I don't see how you can, when the choice be so horrible!"

The princess took a deep breath and drew up her shoulders. "Tess, be still, and button my gown! That is a command!"

The chambermaid sniffed. Her freckled face was pink with outrage. "Yes, miss," she said, and curtsied.

16.

The Banquet

The banquet tables had been set with the finest of the castle's engraved silver flatware and hand-painted china. Masses of flowers had been arranged in crystal vases placed at intervals along the length of each table. Footmen in full uniform stood at attention around the walls, waiting to attend the guests, and serving maids in freshly starched aprons scurried in and out, carrying plates of butter and celery and baskets of fresh-baked breads of all sorts. In the kitchen far below, massive tables held the plates of food, all of it waiting to be lifted up by pulley and served to the guests. The pigeons were creamed, the pistachios shelled, and two hundred artichokes had been stuffed with goose liver and arranged on plates.

In the corridor, the three singing serving girls, exempted from serving duties, were rehearsing their song. They had spent the entire previous night perfecting the rhymes and practicing the harmonies.

"Tonight's the night of the Birthday Ball," they sang.

"Dinner first in the banquet hall," they sang next.

"Banquet hall Banquet hall Banquet hall!" Here their voices divided into a complex harmony and formed a chorus.

"Gifts and fun for one and all . . ."

"Birthday Ball Birthday ball Birthday Ball!"

The elderly serving boy hobbled past them, carrying a fresh case of sardines. "That blasted cat's gone and had kittens. More mouths to feed," he muttered irritably. "Why don't you make up a song about *that?*" He glared at the serving girls in their pinafores. "Plenty of words to rhyme with *cat,* I'd say. *Brat* and *fat* and *drat,* for a few." He continued on his way, muttering.

From the bell tower, suddenly, the sound of the carillon began. Usually it played only the number of the hours, but now it rang a melody to signal the start of the event. The villagers, bathed and dressed in their best, had all been waiting at the gate to the castle grounds for the signal. Now they pushed the gate open and flooded through, the children skipping happily, the older village folk, many of them wearing unaccustomed shoes, trying to walk with dignity and purpose.

From their three encampments on the grounds, the visiting suitors emerged from their tents.

Duke Desmond wore a one-piece form-fitting green outfit, stretched across his pudgy belly and outlining his legs down to the ankles. On his feet he wore pointed green suede shoes with slippery soles that would help him to glide on the dance floor; he had practiced the waltz again and again, back in his own domain, and had created his own version of the dance, using dips and twirls that made his thick cord of hair fly back and forth.

Now, as he walked in a stately fashion toward the castle, surrounded by his courtiers, he did a little hop here and there, holding his arms out, pretending the princess was already encircled in them. He murmured sweet nothings under his breath in preparation, and blew some spit-laden air kisses (not easy to do, around his protruding teeth), relishing the thought that very soon his saliva would be decorating her lovely pink neck.

The splashers scurried ahead of him, rushing to flutter their hands in the castle birdbaths, and behind him came the bearer of the butterfly, carrying the elaborate bamboo cage that housed his gift to the king.

At the same time, from another direction, completely surrounded by mirror bearers walking sideways in the prescribed manner, Prince Percival began strolling toward the castle entrance. He was dressed entirely in black, and had enhanced his eyelashes with jet black mascara and added a little metallic gray shadow above, on the lids.

He was practicing his own dance steps, pointing his toes and wiggling his slim hips in a kind of tango. He turned from left to right, admiring himself in the mirrors as he did, stopping occasionally to check his makeup (for in addition to the mascara and eye shadow, he had applied some blush) or to adjust his mustache. Frequently he ordered another whisking of his shoulders by the valet, who trotted immediately behind him, carrying the dandruff brushes.

He carried his gift in his own back pocket, adjusting it now and then when the mirrors revealed that it was causing an unsightly bulge.

Behind his group, though unseen, a large swarm of bees was following in a slow-moving, purposeful cloud. The ringing of the carillon, which continued playing birthday music, masked the deep buzzing hum.

Finally, the conjoint counts, wearing a red plaid suit that they had finally agreed grudgingly upon, lurched forward from their encampment. They moved in circles because of their disagreements, one turning left while the other turned right, which invariably slowed them down and required a full circle before they could get aimed toward the castle once again.

Cuthbert had combed and trimmed his beard, but Colin had poked him in the ribs while he was doing so, causing the scissors to slip, so the beard now had an oddly scalloped shape. Colin himself had shaved, but Cuthbert had nastily jostled the arm that held the razor several times. So Colin's cheeks and chin were peppered with small dots of blood-smeared toilet paper, which he intended to remove as soon as they reached the castle entrance.

The villagers arrived first and were welcomed and ushered inside, then led up the grand staircase to the banquet hall. Their eyes were wide at the magnificence of the marble floors, the fine tapestries on the walls, and most of all, when the banquet hall doors were pulled open, at the huge tables set with embroidered cloths and decorated with flowers, candles, and plates that hinted at the food yet to be served.

Footmen pulled out individual chairs and helped each villager to be seated. In a corner of the banquet hall, a harp player began to pluck the strings of a magnificent instrument, and the deep, vibrating chords filled the room with background music.

A footman consulted his list and looked down at a very small girl in a patched dress who seemed to be all alone and a little overwhelmed.

He leaned down and said gently, "Might you be Liz?"

She nodded.

"An orphan?" he asked, still looking at his list.

"Yes, that's me, a norphan," she whispered. "I never been to nuffink like this before."

He took her hand. "You're to sit here," he said, indicating a gilt chair, "next to the princess." He lifted the little girl into it and sat her on its satin cushion. She found herself beside the chair of honor, which was still unoccupied.

"Blimey," Liz said aloud. She grinned and scratched her mosquito bite.

The harpist played a long chord and then fell silent, and buglers entered the hall. Standing at either side of the doorway, they waited while a butler called out "Their Majesties!" and then played a fanfare as the king and queen entered.

The king hated parties. He loved his daughter, wished her well on her birthday—in fact, wished for the best for her always—but he hated parties and hoped that this one would not last long. He disliked ceremonies, was uncomfortable in his gold tights, and wanted to get back to his butterfly collection.

The queen, in contrast, adored elaborate occasions. She had spent the entire morning trying on one gown after another, having her hair done and redone, fussing with jewels and makeup, and enjoying time-consuming preparations for her daughter's birthday. Even now, as she entered the banquet hall, nodding her head graciously to the left and right, she was thinking that she should have worn the patent leather shoes with the stiletto heels instead of the soft satin ones she had chosen.

"Would you hold this scepter?" she muttered to the king. "I can't greet everyone graciously with a

stupid scepter in my hand." He took it from her, and she began to blow kisses to the villagers, who had stood respectfully at their seats and were watching their entrance in awe.

"Please, be seated, humble peasants," she called to the long tables lined with standing villagers.

With her husband she walked to the two magnificent chairs waiting for them at one end of the head table. Arranging her skirts, she sat gracefully in one, and the king took his place beside her. The harpist resumed playing.

"What would you like me to do with the scepter?" the king murmured.

"Eh?"

"The *scepter*," he repeated.

"What's kept her? She'll be here. She's going to make an entrance. After the suitors arrive. Look at that, dear! Look at that sweet little waif."

The queen waved to Liz at the far end of the long table.

The king sighed and placed the scepter on the floor under his chair.

"We're ready!" the queen called to the butler at the door. "Bring in the suitors now!"

17.

The Arrivals

The schoolmaster was late. Wearing his best clothes and carrying a small birthday gift, a bouquet of flowers, for the princess, he had joined the throng of villagers at the gate to the castle grounds and waited there for the carillon to announce the beginning of the celebration.

But when the bells began to ring and the crowd moved forward, he lingered. He was looking for his favorite pupil, the young girl, Pat, who had only recently joined his classroom. He had a gift for her, as well. It seemed an appropriate time, this celebratory evening, to present her with a gift that he hoped would trigger a desire in her to go on for further training to become a teacher.

There was something about Pat. She was pretty, of course; he recognized that. But it wasn't her good looks. It was her liveliness, he thought, her energy and enthusiasm, and her love of learning. And, too, the gentleness with which she helped the younger children, especially the tiniest one, the one named Liz. And her sense of humor! He liked that almost most of all, watching her try to keep her face serious, the way he so often did himself, forcing himself to be stern in visage when his mouth wanted to move, always, into a smile.

He looked around. Far ahead, on the castle steps, he could see his fellow villagers lining up to enter. But there was still no sign of Pat. It would soon be too late. The doors would soon close behind the villagers, and he feared he would not have the courage to approach all alone.

He could see, too, three odd processions of foreigners approaching from different directions. They looked like nobility, surrounded by their courtiers, but it was strange, the way they moved, hopping and prancing, and there was not a royal look to any one of them.

She was not coming, he thought miserably. She had decided against coming. He looked down the winding path, but it was empty, and his shoulders slumped in disappointment. So many losses in his life, the schoolmaster thought. His mother's death. The disappearance of his beloved little sister. The day that his father turned his back on him and ordered him out of his life. Each memory flooded through him now as he stood alone at the gate and realized that the lively schoolgirl would not be joining him on this night.

Arrange your face to hide your feelings. That was what he had been taught to do, and he did it now. He straightened up, swallowed to force back the feeling of tears that had surprisingly begun to well in him, set his face in stern lines, and walked forward, all alone, to the castle.

Far below the banquet hall, in the kitchen, the three singing serving girls waited at the foot of the stairs for their signal. They were wearing new embroidered pinafores and were very, very nervous. *Mmmmmmm,* they hummed together very quietly, readying their voices. *Mmmmmmmm.*

In the back corridor, Tess the chambermaid

watched with admiration as the pulley boy lifted tray after tray with a steady grip on the thick rope. The creamed pigeons ascended. Then the carved goats. The artichokes, tray after tray. A line of servants moved each delicacy by assembly line from the kitchen to the pulley. Tess stayed carefully out of their way, but she was astounded at how swiftly and seamlessly everything moved.

"THE VILLAGERS IS IN!" Cook called. She had gotten the word, relayed down the staircase from footmen.

"Now?" the singing girls asked.

"Not yet. Not till they calls for you," Cook said. She retied the sash on the youngest, then patted the starched bow into a perky shape.

Tess watched the muscles in the pulley boy's arms. The heavy task seemed effortless to him. The salmons were moving up now.

"What does the banquet hall look like?" she asked the elderly serving boy, who was in his rocker with a blanket over his arthritic knees.

"You seen above-stairs," he said irritably.

"I've seen the princess's bedchamber," she told him. "That's all."

"All marble and crystal and silver and gold," he said. "Big chandeliers. Chinese vases. Tapestries. Fancy stuff. All needs polishing and tidying all the time."

"Blimey," the chambermaid breathed. "I wish I could see it."

"KING AND QUEEN IS IN!" Cook reported loudly.

"Now?" asked the triplets.

"Not yet. Queen has to blow kisses and such. And there's still the suit— Wait," Cook said, and went to get a message from the footman.

"SUITORS IS IN!" she bellowed.

"Now?" asked the singing girls nervously.

"I *told* you! Not yet! The princess ain't in yet! Wait till they calls you!"

Mmmmmm, they hummed, to calm themselves. *Mmmmmm.*

"Them suitors is horrible," Cook said to everyone. "All the footmen sez so. They seen 'em comin' in."

"Oh, the poor princess," Tess murmured. "And she must choose one tonight.

"I wish I could see," she said again, longingly. "I wish I could watch." But the chambermaid had been ordered to stay below-stairs.

The pulley boy heard her. "Food's all up," he said. "If you want, I could lift you up by the pulley and you could peek."

"By the pulley?" she asked in astonishment.

He grinned. "Sure. I did it fer my brother once, just playin' around. Got him all the way up, no problem. You don't weigh no more than him. No more than a roast goat. I'm strong."

She looked again at his muscular arms and nodded. "I know you are," she whispered.

"PRINCESS IS IN!" Cook shouted. She turned to the singing girls. "Get ready." The trio began to take deep, calming breaths.

A hush fell in the kitchen. The pulley was silent, all the food having been lifted. The cook was silent, waiting for the signal. The singing girls were silent, breathing deeply to assuage their nervousness. The elderly serving boy rocked silently.

Tess tiptoed across the corridor. The pulley boy put his finger to his lips, whispered "Shhh," and helped her into the opening, where carefully she arranged herself on the tray.

"It'll be dark," he whispered, leaning into the place where she now crouched. "And when I start lifting, them ropes'll make a creaking sound. Don't be scairt of it."

"I won't," she whispered back. "I'm very brave, like Alice in the book, and used to odd things."

"*A* fer Alice," he said to her, and grinned.

"*B* fer *brave*," she replied, and he began to pull.

"There's an interruption!" Cook listened attentively for a moment to the message delivered by the footman, then passed it on to the triplets, explaining, "Someone came late. The doors was already shut. But they let him in, so now he has to take his seat. It'll be just another minute."

She waited, listening again, then added, "It's the schoolmaster."

The pulley passage was narrow and very dark, as the pulley boy had explained it would be. Tess, crouching uncomfortably on the tray, found herself holding her breath as she moved slowly upward through the castle walls. The tray swayed and scraped against the stone walls on either side, but the hold on the rope was firm and steady. She felt a small draft as she passed the pulley passage door on the second floor; then, finally, she reached the third, and could hear, far below, the sounds as the pulley boy fastened the rope tightly to secure her there on the dangling tray.

"You all right, then?" He was whispering, but the hollow passage carried the echoing whisper up to her.

"Fine!" she called back. She leaned over the edge and could see a light at the bottom outlining his head in the open pulley passage door far below.

"I'll keep you there till they need to send the empties down!" he called. "But I have to lower you then so's they won't find you!"

"Yes, all right!" Tess called down. Carefully she felt in the darkness for the latch to the door, and opened it a crack very slowly, fearful that someone may be standing near. But all of the servants had lined up at the edge of the banquet hall to watch the ceremony that was about to take place.

She opened the door a little farther and pushed her face against the opening so that she could see. There was the marble floor, which the elderly serving boy had described, and she could see a glimpse of a tapestry on a nearby wall. A delicate silk curtain moved slightly in the breeze from an open window. She noticed a Chinese vase on a small table with curved legs. And if she tilted her head and stretched her neck, she could see a bit of a lavish chandelier above. She was looking into the reception hall just outside the huge room where the banquet was being held.

When she heard familiar giggles and footsteps on the staircase, she ducked back inside, knowing that the triplets had been summoned and were about to appear. Peeking through the open slot, she saw them reach the hallway, enter the banquet hall timidly, holding hands, and assume their position for singing.

She could hear a great deal of commotion from the banquet hall itself. Now that the singing girls had taken their place, there seemed to be no one nearby, so she took a chance, opened the door to its full width, and poked her head out. That way, she could see into the banquet room: the backs of the queen and king, first (she recognized the crowns); many servants, all at attention; many villagers, who seemed to be opening gifts and exclaiming over them.

She could not quite see the princess, who was blocked by several footmen standing at attention near the door, or the people seated around her, which was a disappointment.

But the suitors were visible! And every bit as horrible as she remembered! She leaned forward to examine them one by one just as the king rose, holding a goblet of wine, to make a toast.

The schoolmaster, slumped in the chair to which he'd been assigned after his late arrival, was desolate. He knew he would have to rise and raise his own goblet in a moment, for the king was making a speech that would clearly end in a toast. But it would be a toast to the princess, and he didn't want to participate. He had already dropped the two gifts he had brought onto the floor beneath his chair. The bouquet of flowers that he had picked for the

princess were simple wildflowers, not at all suited for this room or this table or—he groaned inwardly —for this bejeweled, coifed, satin-gowned beauty, the Princess Patricia Priscilla, who had looked at him, her aquamarine eyes alight with admiration but awash, too, with regret, when he arrived.

And his other gift, his gift for Pat, the pupil for whom he had had so much affection and hope? It was abandoned, too, on the floor. For there was no Pat, he realized now. The winsome schoolgirl had simply been the princess, disguised. Why had the princess played such a trick? The schoolmaster felt cheated and duped. It was one more loss in a life that had already been too filled with them.

The king droned on. Something about butterflies, how beautiful they were, like his daughter, the princess, emerging now from the cocoon of child-hood into the blah blah blah. The schoolmaster stopped listening and looked around the lengthy table.

What he saw was very strange. Seated next to his small pupil Liz was a hideous man dressed in green. His head, from which was thrust a thick spikey wad of reddish-brown hair, was on his plate, and he was sobbing loudly.

Liz, he saw to his surprise, was patting the man's cheek and murmuring to him.

The king droned on, and the schoolmaster leaned forward to try to hear what Liz and the hideous man were saying to each other.

"I'm so ugly!" the man wailed. "I never knew!"

"It don't matter," little Liz was saying in a soothing voice.

"I never knew at all until I entered the castle and there was a whole phalanx of courtiers carrying mirrors! *Mirrors!* I never saw one before! I had no idea I was so ugly!" The man burst into fresh tears.

"Stop it," Liz said firmly to him. "I fink you're sweet. It don't matter about ugly."

The man snuffled.

"But you do need to brush your teef," she told him. "And I'll help you wiv that mess of hair."

"You will?" he asked, and lifted his head.

Across the table, the schoolmaster saw another odd sight. A thin man wearing makeup and dressed entirely in black was grabbing utensils, one after another. He had overturned a goblet and a candlestick by reaching frantically across the table to grab things. He was muttering at the same time.

"Wouldn't let my mirror bearers in, eh? No room for a hundred mirror bearers? What kind of domain *is* this? I must see myself! I must *always* see myself!"

He grabbed a silver soup ladle and held it in front of his own face, peering at the bowl of it as he tilted the ladle from side to side. His nose in the image grew huge, then receded to become a miniature nose atop a mammoth lopsided mustache. He had one huge Cyclops eye and one small, slitted piggy one.

"Valet!" he called out desperately. "Someone, summon my valet!"

(But the valet, sensing an opportunity, had slipped through a back door of the hallway and found his way to the kitchen. There he had already introduced himself as Hal to the head housekeeper and applied for the next available job.)

The man in black, while the schoolmaster watched, threw the silver ladle to the floor. From his seat he leaned forward across the table, squinting and mumbling and trying to see his own image in the base of a many-tiered silver candelabra.

With a whoosh of flame it ignited his thick hair lubricant so that for a moment he appeared to have a halo. Then two villagers adroitly doused the flames with their drinking water, and the man sat, defeated, confused, with no eyelashes left, and bald but for a singed fringe around each ear.

"I need my valet," he announced piteously. "I need to have my dandruff whisked."

The elderly peasant woman who had poured water on him glanced sympathetically his way and explained, "Yer gots no dandruff, sir. It's burnt off."

The queen could not hear the bits of commotion at the end of the table. She sat smiling blankly as the king droned on. The king heard nothing but his own voice. He hated parties, hated speeches, hated making toasts. But he did love the princess.

"So," the king concluded. "That's that. Daughter, butterfly. Birthday. And in a minute, a special song, right?" He looked at the triplets. They blushed and nodded.

"And then the choice. The princess makes her choice. Chooses from the suitors, gets a husband. Law of the Domain, that's what it is.

"To the choice!" he said loudly, and held up his goblet.

The guests all rose and echoed the phrase. "To the choice!"

The schoolmaster was beside himself with dismay and disappointment. He rose to his feet out of respect for the king, but he could not bring himself to repeat the words of the toast. Standing silently as the guests raised their glasses to honor the occasion, he glanced at the young woman he had known for such a short and hopeful time as Pat. He wondered whether she felt a disdain for his stupidity, a smugness that he had been so easily fooled.

But to his surprise, he could see that the princess was terribly sad.

The king nodded to the trio of serving maids, and they curtsied together and began their song.

Tess, from her place on the pulley tray, could not see much, but she heard everything. She had listened with a smile to the king's loving words about his daughter, but her face fell when he mentioned the choice and made the toast. How could her beloved princess choose among the three—or four, if the conjoint counts were considered two—equally repulsive suitors?

Tess had heard the duke sobbing, and the orphan's words of comfort. She had glimpsed a tiny bit of the flustered excitement when the prince caught fire. But she couldn't see the conjoint counts. They were seated in a specially built double chair not far from the queen, just out of the chambermaid's range of vision.

She began to hear them mutter, though, when the serving girls began their song.

"What're they, twins like us?" Colin poked his brother and pointed to the serving girls.

Cuthbert poked back. "Quit it!" He leaned forward to get a better view. "Nah. Not twins. There's three of 'em!"

"Are they joint?" Colin asked.

"Nah. Holding hands."

"We can sing as good as that, I bet. We're joint."

"Shhh!" The villagers held their fingers to their mouths. "We want to hear the song."

The counts both put their tongue between their lips in order to make their usual rude noise. But they forgot to. Their attention was caught by the trio, who had begun their song.

"*Tonight's the night of the Birthday Ball,*" they sang.

"*Ball,*" said Count Colin aloud. But he wasn't saying it to be rude. He was—well, he was singing the word along with the girls.

"*Dinner first in the banquet hall,*" they sang next.

"*Hall,*" sang Colin and Cuthbert together.

"*Banquet hall Banquet hall Banquet hall!*"

"We can't do that part 'cuz we only got two of us, blast it all," Colin muttered to his brother.

The girls now performed a special chorus they had rehearsed, to go between each verse. It had no words, just a lyrical melody that they hummed in harmony.

Hummmmm. Hummmmm. Hummmmm.

Count Colin elbowed his brother. *"Bummmmm,"* he sang, and raised an eyebrow naughtily.

"Don't," Count Cuthbert said. *"Bum* is rude."

"But—"

"And *butt* is rude, too! Stop it! Sing right!"

They were both silent for a moment, but one of the triplets glanced over at them and grinned. So the conjoint counts began to sing. They sang in harmony, one tenor, one bass; the three girls felt their way into the same harmony, and they completed the song together. The audience applauded. The three girls curtsied, and the counts lumbered awkwardly to their feet, and bowed, side by side.

"Now," said the king, when the applause subsided, "the gifts from the suitors, and the choice."

18.
The Choice

"Wipe your nose," the orphan instructed.

They had announced the Duke of Dyspepsia first. Obediently he took the napkin the little girl had handed him and wiped his streaming eyes and nose.

"Hold my hand?" he implored. Gently she placed her small hand in his, and he stood. He had entirely forgotten the speech he had intended to make. Something about how the princess would be lucky to have him? Had that really been what he had planned to say?

"I'm Duke Desmond," he said, and sniffed back fresh tears. The little girl squeezed his hand. "Duke of Dyspepsia," he added.

"Ugliest man in the world!" he wailed.

Liz stood up. "Is not!" she said loudly. "He only needs sumbody to take care of him and make him brush his teef every single day! He's *nice!* And he brung a nice gift, too!

"Show it!" she told the weeping duke.

He wiped his eyes again, leaned down, and lifted the small bamboo cage that he had placed under his chair. The guests leaned forward in their seats, trying to see what might be inside the cage.

"I can't hear a word he's saying," the queen said irritably. "What's that he's holding?"

"Shhh," said the king. "It's a cage of some sort."

"Tell about it," Liz whispered to the duke. "Speak up nice and loud!"

So the duke, choking back tears, for he could not stop thinking about how ugly he felt, explained how he had sent searchers for the rarest of butterflies as a gift to the king in exchange for the hand of his daughter.

"And this one came from Africa," he said. "I forget how to say its name. *Chara* . . . Well, something."

"*Charaxes acraeoides?*" The king was on his feet.

"That's it," the duke replied. "Look!" He lifted

the small golden latch and opened the door of the bamboo cage. An amber-colored butterfly with black decorations on its wings fluttered free.

"Blimey, it's beautiful!" the little girl said. "And lookit it go!"

The rare butterfly, the most powerful flier in the Congo, swooped the length of the huge head table, circled the head of the amazed king, lifted itself into a long upward glide, and disappeared through the open window.

"That were sumfink to see!" Liz exclaimed, clapping her hands.

The king, his mouth open, sat back down slowly. "It's gone," he said.

Duke Desmond, still holding Liz's hand, sat down as well. "Yes," he said. "Free."

The queen tapped her crystal water glass with a silver knife to order quiet. She had not understood much of what had just occurred. "Next?" she called.

The thin bald man in black stood up slowly. "I am Percival," he said, "Prince of Pustula." He picked up a butter knife, held it in front of his face, and examined what he saw. No mustache. No hair. He felt destroyed.

"I brought a gift," he announced. "But it is useless now."

He reached into his back pocket, removed the small silver box, and tossed it toward the place where the princess sat. "Here," he said contemptuously. "Do what you want with it. I'm so out of here."

Then he stalked from the room and they could all hear his footsteps as he descended the staircase.

Curiously the princess reached for the container.

She opened its lid, looked in, chuckled, and removed the gift. It was a pair of mirrored glasses, the frames encrusted with diamonds. She reached across the table and handed them to the orphan. "Try them on," she suggested. "They might be fun."

Liz unfolded the glasses and balanced them over her ears and nose. She giggled. "Everyfink's dark!" she said. "But I can see you!" she added, turning to the duke.

He looked at her, saw himself reflected, and burst into tears again.

"You stop that right now!" Liz said. "You just get used to it! Becuz I'm goin' to put these spectacles on every day and you can see your teef gettin' better and better iffen you start brushing regular!"

"Every day? But I'm going back to my own domain—"

"And you be takin' me wiv you! 'Cuz I'm a norphan and got no home!"

"You'd go with an ugly thing like me?" he asked in surprise.

"Iffen you let me bring a kitten," Liz replied with a grin.

The queen tapped again on the crystal glass.

"This is all going on much too long," she announced. "There is still dancing planned. Can we have the final suitor at once?"

But amazingly, the conjoint counts refused to come forward. They were in the corner with the triplets, quietly practicing harmonies, planning new five-part songs.

Hmmmm.
Hmmmm.
Hmmmm.
Hmmmm.
Hmmmm.

"Counts?" the queen called. "We're ready for your presentation now!"

Count Cuthbert looked over. "We're busy," he replied.

"Father? Mother? Villagers?"

The princess, who had been seated and silent, rose from her chair. Everyone turned toward her end of the table. Liz put on her new spectacles and looked up at the princess with a grin. "Not now, Liz," the princess admonished her with a smile.

From her perch on the pulley tray, Tess leaned forward. Soon, she knew, she would be lowered. But she wanted to hear this moment, to know whom the princess would choose.

"It is the moment for the choice," the princess said to the waiting gathering.

"Eh?" The queen could not hear her daughter. "What did she say?" she asked the king.

"The choice. She's making the choice." The king was preoccupied with his own plans. If he could get out to the meadow, and if that *Charaxes acraeoides* had lingered there . . . Well, there was a chance . . .

"I know it is required," the princess went on, and for a moment her voice faltered. "It is the Law of the Domain. Isn't that right, Father?"

The king nodded. He looked at his watch and yearned for the evening to end. "Law of the Domain."

"And only you can change that?" The princess felt this was her only hope: convincing her father, even at this last moment, that he must change the Law of the Domain. "You being king, I mean?"

The king was startled. His daughter was correct. But the procedure for changing the Law of the

Domain was complex and lengthy and very, very time-consuming. "Yes," he acknowledged. "Only I. Being king. Very time-consuming. Minimum, seven years."

The princess's heart sank. *Seven years?* She'd be *old* by then! She didn't want to wait seven years!

"Well," she said, frantically searching in her mind for another solution, "am I correct, also, that the princess—that's me, of course." Here she laughed nervously. "Ah, the princess has to choose a husband, and he must be nobility?"

"Nobility. Correct. Prince. Duke. Count. Whatever." The king groaned inwardly, suffering for his daughter. The hideous duke was slobbering in his seat and being comforted by a waif. The repulsive prince had fled, stopping only briefly to squat and look at himself in a highly polished doorknob, and a footman had whispered to the king that he was now being pursued around the castle grounds by bees. The counts, one of them with toilet paper stuck in wads all over his face, were singing madrigals in a far corner with the serving maids.

The princess took a deep breath. "All right, then, I'm ready. I will make the choice."

The room fell absolutely silent.

The princess remembered, in that instant, what the schoolmaster had said to her once: *You are tall and slender as a young willow tree, supple and lovely.* She drew herself up and stood very straight.

"I choose to marry Herr Gutmann," she said.

19.

The Happy Ending

"What did she say? What did my daughter say? I demand to know what the princess said!" The queen turned to her husband.

"She said something that makes no sense," he explained to her, enunciating clearly. "She said she wants to marry someone named Herr Gutmann!"

"The footman? Impossible!" the queen gasped.

"No, not the footman! *Herr Gutmann* is what she said!"

Around the table, all of the villagers were murmuring the same word. *Impossible. Impossible. Impossible.*

"It *isn't* impossible!" the princess, near tears, in-

sisted. "My chambermaid told me about Herr Gutmann! He's nobility! He just likes to *pretend* to
peasanthood! But he's truly noble, and qualifies!"

From her hiding place in the pulley passage, Tess
listened, and her eyes grew wide. The princess had
chosen the schoolmaster? That stern, bearded man
who had taught her to read and sometimes rapped
her knuckles with a ruler? He was old! But still,
perhaps it was better than the horrible suitors!

A tall peasant woman, wringing and twisting
her hands in nervousness on her skirt, stood.
"Please, Your Majesties? Please, Princess? I can explain why it's impossible."

"Do so, then," the king commanded. He sighed.
It was dark now outside. This was all taking much
too long. The butterfly was out there somewhere.

"Herr Gutmann *is* nobility, it is true," the peasant woman explained. "That is, he *was*. Oh, I suppose he still *is*. Oh dear, I'm very nervous."

"Get to the point!" the king said.

"Well, the point being, Herr Gutmann went back
to his own domain these many months ago, where
he married his old friend Gertrude, her being a
widow and all. He can't marry twice, not even if

the princess chooses him!" The peasant woman sat down and bowed her head in embarrassment. She had never spoken in public before.

"No!" cried the princess. "He's not old! Not married! He's here! He's right here! Look! I brought him a book!" She held out the gift she had saved for the schoolmaster, the book of maps, and read the inscription aloud: "'For Herr Gutmann, with thanks from Patricia Priscilla, who was Pat for too short a time.' But he hasn't looked at me all evening, and I think my heart will break!" She pointed to the young schoolmaster.

He looked up at her and put it together in his mind, what she had thought, and how it was all hopeless. He stood.

He said slowly, "I too have brought a gift." He reached under his chair and held up exactly the same book of maps. He read his own inscription: "'For my dear pupil Pat.' But there has been such a misunderstanding. You are not my dear pupil Pat. She doesn't exist. And I am not Herr Gutmann. I am the new schoolmaster, only come recently from the teachers' academy.

"And," he went on, "I am truly a poor peasant,

not nobility at all, so my heart is breaking, too.

"My name is Rafe," he said.

"Rafe!" Tess, on hearing the name, tumbled in a twirl of petticoats out of the pulley passage, onto the marble floor. "Ow!" she said. "Bruised me bum, I did!" Then she picked herself up and ran forward into the banquet hall. She found the schoolmaster, threw her arms around him, and grinned at the princess. "It's me brother, miss! The one I thought was gone forever!"

"Tess? My little lost sister? Pa sent you to work at the castle?" Rafe replied in delight as he hugged the freckled chambermaid.

"I'm happy for you both," the princess told them. And she was. But she was terribly sad for herself.

"Explain to me what is happening," the queen said to the king. "That's quite a good-looking man there, but he's wrapped his arms around the seventeenth chambermaid, and I don't like that one bit!"

"Sister. Long lost."

"And our daughter? Did she make the choice or not? I couldn't hear a thing. It seemed as if she was choosing a footman. We can't have that. All this hugging of servants! Quite unthinkable! And she looks sad."

The king leaned close to his wife. "Schoolmaster, dear. The good-looking one. She chose him. Can't happen. Not nobility. Very sad."

"Not nobility?"

"No. Not."

"What's his name?"

"Rafe, he says."

"*Treif?* That's a terrible name!"

"It's *Rafe!*" the king said loudly.

"Rafe!" the queen called. "Rafe, pay attention here! Disentangle yourself from the chambermaid! I'm summoning you! Come forward!" She made a summoning gesture with her hand toward the schoolmaster.

"You must obey when she summons," Tess whispered to her brother. She pushed him forward.

The queen had lifted her skirts and was looking around the floor by her feet. "Where's my stupid scepter?" she asked. "You always put things where I can't find them!"

The king crouched by his chair, searched the

carpet, and found the jeweled scepter where it had rolled near the feet of a peasant. "Here," he said, and gave it to the queen.

"Kneel, Rafe!" the queen commanded. Then she called to her daughter. "You come up here and watch, dear! I hate seeing you so sad!"

The princess gathered her skirts and came to stand beside her parents. The schoolmaster, brow furrowed, was kneeling there obediently.

"I'm going to make you nobility," the queen explained, "but you need more of a name. Rafe is very peasant-y. You need to be Rafe the . . .

"Any ideas?" the queen asked the entire gathering. "It has to start with an *R*!"

The little orphan, who was just learning to read, made the sound to herself, thinking hard. "*Rrrrr*. Rafe the Ridiculous? No, I don't fink so." She giggled.

"Repellent?" suggested Duke Desmond. "No, that's *me*." But he grinned down at Liz.

"Redoubtable?" proposed the king. "No. Not good."

The chambermaid came forward. "Please, miss?" she said to the princess, with a curtsy.

"Do you want to be nobility, too, Tess?" the princess asked sympathetically. "Mother, could you possibly—"

"Oh, no, miss! Not at all!" The freckled face had turned pink. "'Cuz the pulley boy, he ain't nobility, and—"

"What, then?" The princess worried that it was a long time for the schoolmaster to be balanced on his knee, and he might be uncomfortable.

"I wanted to say: *Remarkable.* That's what he is, my brother. Always was."

The princess smiled, and said it loudly to her mother. "REMARKABLE."

So the queen touched the scepter to the schoolmaster's shoulders, one after the other, and named him as a knight. "Sir Rafe the Remarkable! Rise!"

He rose, newly knighted. "There, Sir Rafe," the queen said. "Now you're nobility. That was easy. Let's forget dinner. Let the dancing begin!" At her command, the royal orchestra, which had been waiting for the signal, began to play in the ballroom, and the doors were opened to reveal the polished floor that waited.

Sir Rafe took the hand of the princess and

smiled at her. "This has been a very confusing evening, Princess . . ."

"Please call me Pat," she told him. "I loved being Pat."

"Very well, Pat. But I am still a bit mystified. You seem to have chosen me. Chosen me for what?"

The princess laughed. "First of all, to help me become a teacher, of course!" She took his hand and led him onto the ballroom floor. "After that? Well, we'll see." She waited, listening to the music, for him to place her arm around her waist.

He stood there, embarrassed. "I don't know how to dance," he confessed, blushing.

"Ah!" she replied in delight, and reached out her arms to show him how to arrange his. "My first teaching assignment!"

The Happy End.